PRAISE FOR

LEMON

"A taut novella . . . told so vividly and poetically . . . Kwon pulls off what I can describe only as a sleight of hand . . . Her sentences are crisp, concise, and potent; just one contains as much meaning as two or three of your average storyteller's . . . You'll wish there were more; but you'll be grateful it ended as it did . . . a bright, intense, refreshing story."

—Oyinkan Braithwaite, *New York Times Book Review*

"An idiosyncratic and beguiling mystery . . . *Lemon* surveys the damage wrought by a single heinous act on a number of interconnected lives, and does so with impressive deftness."   —*The Spectator*

"Kwon's brief, fierce novel takes daring leaps through time . . . A chilling examination of the repercussions of violence."   —*Kirkus Reviews*

"Chilling, suspenseful, and disconcerting. A story of taking things into one's own hands, when driven to despair by injustice and grief. I couldn't put it down and read deep into the night until I finished it, with my heart hammering."

—Frances Cha, author of *If I Had Your Face*

"A confounding masterpiece, *Lemon* is a meditation on grief, death, beauty, God, and art, wrapped in the mourning clothes of a murder mystery. One of the most profound page-turners you will ever encounter, and the first English translation of a major Korean author who should be on everyone's radar."

—Matthew Salesses, author of *Craft in the Real World*

"I found this book charming, beguiling, and unique. At the heart of this 'mystery' is a poetic meditation on grief, guilt, and the meaning of life. In the end, *Lemon*, like a great painting, makes you see the world differently."

—Patrick Hoffman, author of *Clean Hands* and *Every Man a Menace*

"Kwon Yeo-sun's *Lemon* is a gripping mystery with an eccentric and thought-provoking edge. It's quite the unputdownable read!"

—June Hur, author of *The Silence of Bones* and *The Forest of Stolen Girls*

"*Lemon* opens with the death of a high school student but Kwon Yeo-sun quickly cracks open the secret rivalries between teenage girls to reveal an unending silent scream of loneliness, cruelty, and nihilism that goes on to permeate their adult lives. What a jet-black switchblade of a book!"

—Sandi Tan, director of *Shirkers*
and author of *Lurker*s

"*Lemon* is a deliciously rewarding novel that delves into assumptions about power, wealth, beauty, love, ability, and right to compensation. How well do we know each other? How do we move on from violent loss? I'm in awe of Kwon's gorgeous prose and intricately crafted mystery at the heart of this elegant thriller."

—Jimin Han, author of *A Small Revolution*

LEMON

KWON YEO-SUN

Translated from the Korean by Janet Hong

Other Press / New York

First softcover edition 2022
ISBN 978-1-63542-331-0

Originally published in Korean as 레몬 [Lemon]
in 2019 by Changbi Publishers, Inc., Seoul
Copyright © 2019 Kwon Yeo-sun
Translation copyright © 2021 Janet Hong

This book is published with the support of the Literature
Translation Institute of Korea (LTI Korea).

Production editor: Yvonne E. Cárdenas
Text designer: Jennifer Daddio / Bookmark Design & Media Inc.
This book was set in Cochin and Lettres Eclatees

1 3 5 7 9 10 8 6 4 2

Library of Congress Cataloging-in-Publication Data
Names: Kwŏn, Yŏ-sŏn, 1965- author. | Hong, Janet, translator.
Title: Lemon / Kwon Yeo-sun ; translated from the Korean by Janet Hong.
Description: New York : Other Press, 2021.
Identifiers: LCCN 2021006077 (print) | LCCN 2021006078 (ebook) |
ISBN 9781635420883 (hardcover) | ISBN 9781635420890 (ebook)
Classification: LCC PL994.46.Y67 L4513 2021 (print) | LCC PL994.46.Y67 (ebook) |
DDC 895.73/5—dc23
LC record available at https://lccn.loc.gov/2021006077
LC ebook record available at https://lccn.loc.gov/2021006078

Publisher's Note
This is a work of fiction. Names, characters, places,
and incidents either are the product of the author's imagination
or are used fictitiously, and any resemblance to actual
persons, living or dead, events, or locales is entirely coincidental.

CONTENTS

SHORTS, 2002

●

I IMAGINE what happened inside one police interrogation room so many years ago. By *imagine*, I don't mean *invent*. But it's not like I was actually there, so I don't know what else to call it. I picture the scene from that day, based on what he told me and some other clues, my own experience and conclusions. It's not just this scene I imagine. For over sixteen years, I've pondered, prodded, and worked every detail embroiled in the case known as "The High School Beauty Murder"—to the point I often fool myself into thinking I'd personally witnessed the circumstances now stamped on my mind's eye. The imagination is just as painful as reality. No, it's more painful. After all, what you imagine has no limit or end.

THE BOY sat alone in the interrogation room for over ten minutes. The room was bare apart from a table and four chairs. No pictures decorated the wall, no flower vase or ashtray sat on the table. Some people appear uneasy no matter what they do, and this boy was one of them. He sat awkwardly in his chair, with eyes dull and sleepy-looking. Maybe because there was nothing to look at, but his eyes were like camera lenses constantly shifting to find focus on a white background.

A detective entered the room and sat across from the boy. The boy's gaze grew a bit more focused.

"Han Manu!" the detective snapped, in a tone used by a teacher or head disciplinarian to summon a troublemaker before dealing out punishment.

It was enough for resentment to take root in the boy's heart. I believe this was also the moment his cruel fate was sealed.

At the time, no one at school called him by his actual name. The other students called him *Halmanggu* or *Manujeol*, but his most shining nickname came from the song "Han-o-baeg-nyeon."* To their ears, the opening words "ha-an-man-eu-eu-eun" sounded just like his name. If you slurred the *n* sound so that you said "ha-an-man-*u-u-u*" instead, it was perfect. This particular nickname proved so popular that both *Halmanggu* and *Manujeol* died out eventually, and his friends would belt out "Ha-an man-u-u-u!" like a master pansori singer, warming up her voice before a performance.

But until the incident, I wasn't even aware of his existence. He was in his last year of senior high and I'd just entered the school. When I grope through my memory, though, I seem to recall boys warbling his name in a ridiculous, plaintive way in the halls. They meant no harm or disrespect. After the incident, the nickname stopped altogether. No one called him anything. There was no need.

I sometimes try calling him the old way. *Ha-an man-u-u-u.* This life full of misery, as the lyrics say. Then I start wondering if this miserable life has any meaning. I don't mean life in an abstract or general

---

* The translation of *halmanggu* is *bag*, and *manujeol* is *April Fool's Day.* "Han-o-baeg-nyeon" is a famous Korean folk song. Translated as "Five-hundred-year Sorrow," the song became a big hit when singer Cho Yong-pil released it in his 1979 debut album.

sense, but the life of an actual person. Did the pages of his life hold any meaning? Probably not. At least that's what I believe. Life has no special meaning. Not his, not my sister's, not even mine. Even if you try desperately to find it, to contrive some kind of meaning, what's not there isn't there. Life begins without reason and ends without reason.

THE DETECTIVE told the boy to listen carefully: this was different from last time, he needed to think carefully before answering; if not, things wouldn't go well for him. The detective's face was curiously blank. Though the boy wasn't the brightest kid on the block, he could sense the older man had become more frightening than he'd been at the initial questioning. He seethed with something, and anyone seething like that was to be feared.

"Let's start by reviewing your statement from last time. On June 30, 2002, around 18:00," the detective said, punctuating his words by pressing the tip of his ballpoint pen carefully on the table. "That is, around six o'clock in the afternoon, you were on your scooter on your way to a chicken delivery when you passed a car being driven by Shin Jeongjun. Correct?"

"No."

"No?" The detective's gaze skimmed the document and shot back up. "Well, that's what your statement says."

"I wasn't on my way to a delivery. I was on my way back."

An inconsequential detail. The detective looked down once more.

"Then why does it say here you were going to a delivery? Fine, whatever. So you were on your way back when you passed a car that Shin Jeongjun was driving? Correct?"

"Yes."

"What kind of car did you say it was?"

"Pardon me?"

"The car model!" He was sure the boy was just pretending not to understand. "What kind of car was he driving?"

"Uh, I'm not sure, but I think it was dark gray. And shiny. Didn't I mention all this last time?"

"I told you, we're going over your statement. So a shiny dark gray car?"

"Yes."

"Like this?"

The detective pulled out a photo from the file. The boy leaned forward, peered at the photo, and looked up.

"I don't know. Maybe."

"Even if it wasn't this exact one, would you say it was the same kind—an SUV?"

The boy studied the photo once more and looked up at the detective. "I think so."

"For the last time, was it an SUV or not?

"Yes."

"Okay. You're doing good."

The detective pulled out another photo. The boy looked at it and then at the detective's face.

"Is this your scooter?" the detective asked.

The boy responded immediately that it was.

"Good."

The detective riffled through the pages of the file, delaying the moment of the decisive blow.

"Now for the important part. You said you saw Kim Hae-on sitting in the passenger seat of Shin Jeongjun's car, correct?"

"Yes."

"And what did you say again about her hair and her clothes?"

"Her hair was down."

"You mean it was loose, not tied up."

"Yes."

"And? What was she wearing?"

"Um...she was in a tank top and shorts."

"A tank top and shorts?"

"Well, that's what I—"

"What you remember? So what color?"

"Color?"

"Her clothes!" the detective barked, thinking idiots like this never gave a straight answer. "What color were they?"

"I don't know."

"You don't remember?"

"Well, I'm not too sure."

"You know she was in a tank top and shorts, but you don't know what color? You think that makes sense?"

"But I swear I don't know!"

The boy was hiding something. The detective wondered if the time had finally come to nab him. Right then, the boy glanced around the room.

"What's the matter?" the detective asked.

"Um, I have to go."

"What?"

"Do you know what time it is? I have to go to work."

The boy placed his hands on the table, as if he meant to get up. The detective glared at him in silence. What did he think then? Did he think: Got you, asshole! Was it then that he became convinced of the boy's guilt? Or did he glance at the boy's hands on the table, and try to determine if they were capable of clutching something like a brick or rock and bringing it down on someone's head? He might have thought with a shake of his head, Hmm, those hands do look tougher than Shin Jeongjun's. Not that you need a whole lot of power to bash in the small head of a girl with smooth, glossy hair. If anything, Shin Jeongjun was taller, with a body hardened by sports, while Han Manu was rather small and of average height.

The detective cleared his throat and told the boy to pay attention. "Your statement doesn't add up. Look here."

He turned the photos around to face the boy, and proceeded to explain: Shin Jeongjun wasn't driving just any car, but a Lexus RX300. The seat height of an SUV is higher than that of the average sedan, which means its window height is also higher. But if you're sitting on a scooter, you would be at eye level with the window of the SUV, or even slightly lower.

The detective asked if he knew what all this meant. The boy didn't respond. The detective was kind enough to spell it out for him.

"What I'm saying is, from your stumpy little scooter, it would have been physically impossible to see if Kim Hae-on was wearing shorts or jeans."

So he said, but he wasn't completely sure. It was just a hunch. But when he saw the shock on the boy's face, the detective knew it was time to go in for the kill.

"Therefore, you didn't actually see Kim Hae-on in Shin Jeongjun's car. You saw her out of it. That's how you knew she was wearing shorts. You saw Shin dropping her off, or you saw her walking by herself, after he'd dropped her off. Either way, you never saw her sitting in the passenger seat. If we follow that logic..."

The boy blinked several times. Though he heard what the detective was saying, he didn't seem to comprehend the situation he was in. On the detective's lips hovered the nervous smile of one who was about to land a fatal blow.

"The last person to see Kim Hae-on wasn't Shin Jeongjun, but you. Do you understand what I'm saying?"

The boy could only stare. Once again, the detective got the sense that the boy was feigning ignorance. He needed to come out a lot stronger.

"What I'm saying is, you're the prime suspect. You killed Kim Hae-on. You struck her with a blunt object and killed her."

"Me?" the boy cried with a shudder. "But why?"

The boy, who appeared awkward no matter what he did, seemed as if he were acting. The detective became convinced the imbecile couldn't do anything right.

"Weren't you listening? You killed Kim Hae-on and then tried to pin it on Shin Jeongjun, passing yourself off as a witness. Isn't that right?"

"No, of course not! Why would I do that? Why would I kill her?"

"How would I know? You tell me."

"But I've never even spoken to Hae-on! She hardly said a word!"

"Says who?"

"Everyone! She never answered you even when you talked to her. Not that I ever tried or anything."

What the boy said was true, but the detective had zero interest in these seemingly irrelevant details.

"What hogwash is this? Didn't you say she was in shorts? Didn't you see her in them? Tell me how that's possible."

The detective leaned across the table. He wondered how the fool was going to get himself out of this one.

"I don't know...," the boy mumbled, but the detective, intoxicated by his sense of victory, was unable to hear the rest of what he said.

"Oh, you don't know now? You're changing your tune?"

"I'm not saying that..."

"No?"

"I think maybe...uh...maybe somebody else saw it, too."

"Somebody else?"

The boy closed his mouth. He no longer felt like talking. In fact, he was wishing he could take back what he'd just said.

"I don't think you grasp the seriousness of your situation. You're not going to weasel your way out of this. Until now, you said you were the only one who saw Kim Hae-on, so what the hell do you mean by somebody else?"

"I never said I was the only one who saw her."

"You never said that? Fine then. Who else?"

"Do I have to say? I really don't want to."

Manu wouldn't have wanted to tell. He would have hated to bring her up. He would have recalled the warmth of her body from that day, as she'd sat lightly pressed up against his back. Recalling that sensation, he might have grinned like an idiot before the detective, just as he had done with me.

"Have you lost your frigging mind?" The detective wanted to smack the boy's ugly long face that resembled a pickle. "You think this is a joke? You realize you're contradicting yourself, don't you? You'd better fess up—who else saw Kim Hae-on?"

The boy's upper lip twitched. "Um..."

The detective leaned closer. Someone with the last name of Um?

"Um...I've gotta go. Really."

The detective felt his energy drain from him. The boy was absolutely maddening, with an uncanny knack for getting under his skin. Was something really the matter with him? Or was he only pretending to be stupid?

"You're not leaving until you tell me the truth. I don't care if it takes all night. I don't care if it takes forever."

"But my boss needs me. I really have to go—"

"Who else saw?"

The boy mumbled something under his breath.

"Speak up!" the detective roared.

"It was...uh...Taerim," he said, a fleck of spittle flying out of his mouth.

"Taerim?"

"Yun...Yun Taerim."

"Who the hell's Yun Taerim?"

"From Division 3. The same class as Hae-on."

"And this Taerim is female?"

Confusion passed over the boy's face. "Of course. Division 3 is a girls' class."

How in the world was he supposed to know that? He then realized the boy had just mentioned she was in the same class as Kim Hae-on. A wave of anger surged through him.

"Why would you leave out something so important until now? You know what you've done? You've committed perjury. I could put you away for this! I swear to God, if you don't tell me everything from now on, you're in deep shit. Were you with Yun Taerim that day?"

"Yes."

The detective felt as though he'd been clobbered over the head.

"Why were you together?"

"Because Taerim asked for a ride."

"On what? Your scooter?"

"Yes."

"You're killing me, Manu! Are you saying she was on your scooter with you? I thought you were going to—I mean, coming back from a delivery!"

"I was on my way back when I saw her on the street. She waved me over, so I pulled up, and then she asked for a ride. She said it was urgent."

"So you two were on the scooter together and that's when you saw Shin Jeongjun's car?"

"I didn't even know it was his car—uh, his sister's car, I mean. Taerim said his sister had just gotten it, but Jeongjun was driving it around. She told me to get in front."

"In front?"

"Yeah, when we stopped at a red light. She told me to get in front of it."

"In front of what?"

"Jeongjun's car."

"Why'd she say that?"

"I don't know."

"So did you?"

"Yup."

The detective's frustration built. The strange way the boy had of contradicting himself was getting on his nerves, and he found himself tripping over his own tongue.

"And then?"

"So that's why."

"That's why what?"

"That's why Taerim might have seen."

Taerim might have seen. To the detective, these words would have sounded like a lie, but they confirmed the truth for me. Yun Taerim would have wanted to know who was in the passenger seat of Shin Jeongjun's car. She would have gotten on Han Manu's scooter, telling him to get in front of it. This detail contained a subtle truth the boy would never have been able to invent on his own.

"Why the hell didn't you mention this last time?"

"Because...I didn't think she liked it."

"Didn't like what?"

"The scooter."

"What are you talking about?"

"Taerim didn't like it."

"Come again?"

"Riding the scooter."

"You're saying she didn't like riding your scooter?"

"That's right."

"Why'd you give her a ride then?"

"Because she asked me. She was the one who waved me over. I never asked if she wanted a ride!"

"You didn't ask her, fine. But why would you give her a ride if she didn't want to get on your scooter? And why didn't you say anything until now?"

"You don't understand, Mister. She'd never get on something like that."

The detective felt as if he were about to lose his mind.

"Okay, let me get this straight. It's not that you didn't want to give Taerim a ride, but she doesn't like scooters and would never get on something like that. Is that what you're saying?"

"She wouldn't be caught dead on a delivery scooter. So imagine how shocked I was when she asked for a ride! Then she said she wanted to get off, so I dropped her off. That means she didn't like it, doesn't it?"

"She asked you to drop her off right away? What was so urgent then?"

"Urgent?"

"You said she waved you over and asked for a ride, because it was urgent."

"Oh, I didn't ask why."

Was there ever such an idiot? the detective thought.

A stupid detective wouldn't have figured it out, but if a girl, who's ashamed of being seen on a scooter, asks an idiot boy for a ride on his delivery scooter and then tells him to pass Shin Jeongjun's car, only to get off immediately, isn't the reason obvious? She was simply trying to see who Shin Jeongjun was with. After confirming my sister's presence in the car, Taerim had promptly gotten off the scooter. What exactly had she seen at that moment? How beautiful my sister looked? How indifferent? How cruel?

THE DETECTIVE shook his head. His belief that this moron was guilty remained unshaken; he knew the boy was trying to take the negative attention off himself by dragging in a girl named Yun Taerim, but he was just digging himself into a bigger hole.

"Han Manu, I know you're lying."

"I swear it's the truth! But I really have to go."

"You're lying, one hundred percent. You realize I'm going to bring Yun Taerim in for questioning, don't you? Before deciding to lie, you should have gotten your story straight. How in the world would Yun Taerim manage to see something you couldn't see? Let's say she saw Kim Hae-on in a tank top with her hair down, but how could she have seen anything else? Is she taller than you? Even if she's taller, she still wouldn't have been able to see what Kim Hae-on was wearing on the bottom. It's physically impossible."

"I really gotta go," the boy said sullenly.

"You listening with your ass? For the hundredth time, from your crappy midget scooter, there's no way you could have seen Kim Hae-on in shorts. Got that?"

"All right."

"All right? That's all you have to say? Are you admitting you're wrong?"

"No, but..."

The detective leaned across the table, sensing that victory was at hand.

"Mister, could you not call it a midget scooter?"

The detective gave a humorless laugh. "I'm going to ask you one last time. You're saying, since you saw Kim Hae-on in shorts, Yun Taerim must have seen, too?"

"Yes."

"I'll be looking into this. If it turns out you're lying, you're dead."

"Can I go now?"

"You can go."

Frowning, the detective watched the boy get up from his seat, bow, and make his way out of the interrogation room, his sneakers dragging along the floor. He would have fallen into thought then, tapping the documents on the table, lining up the corners and edges. I'm aware of this habit. Just as I'm aware of his other habits, of placing a stack of paper on the table and pressing it hard with the tip

18

of his retracted pen, scattering the pages he had just straightened. Even now, I can recall his facial expressions and manner of speaking, his squat neck atop a stocky frame, which made him resemble a gorilla. Many times he had come to our apartment, and many times I'd gone to the station with my mother.

That day, the detective would have weighed Han Manu's narrow, pinched face against Shin Jeongjun's clean features, the former's cheap World Cup T-shirt against the latter's IVYclub button-down shirt, a single mother against an accountant father, and the twentieth rank in class against the top ten of the entire grade, as well as the credibility of the witnesses providing the alibis. Rather than try to find the real culprit, the detective would have considered whom he could—or should—crush and turn into the culprit. And that's exactly what he tried to do.

I'VE BEEN constructing this second interrogation in my mind for a long time, the way you might put LEGO pieces together. Han Manu was questioned a total of seven times, but it was this interview that hinted at the truth, and the way the case would eventually unfold. Yet, the strange thing was, each time I re-created the second interview, an excess of details would emerge. As if small, warped pieces of LEGO were finding their way in, somehow. This had nothing to do with Han Manu or the detective. It was my problem.

It happened again this time. I'd written that the detective, as he gazed at Han Manu's hands, thought a person doesn't need a whole lot of power to bash in the small head of a girl with smooth glossy hair. Why had such an unnecessary detail intruded into the scene? A small head, fine, but hair that's smooth and glossy has no bearing on the way someone is struck. The detective would have never added such a useless detail while questioning a suspect. Of course my sister's dazzling beauty, clearly displayed even by her lifeless body, may have crossed his mind all of a sudden. It doesn't matter if he imagined these things or not. The problem is that this kind of excess keeps slipping into that imagined scene. What I've done is project my own thoughts and desires onto the detective. Does this mean I'm still not free? That I'm not free, not one iota, from those smooth, fair, irrelevant details from sixteen years ago, those endless memories of my sister's loveliness, which had made me undergo plastic surgery, turning my own face into a crude patchwork of her features?

It's true. My sister was beautiful. Unforgettably so. She was perfection, bliss personified. But more than anything, she was at that mythical age: eighteen. Who dared destroy her lovely form? Was it Han Manu, Shin Jeongjun, or a third figure? Now I know—not who killed my sister, but who didn't. No, that's not true. I know who the murderer is. That's why I did what I did, and I know I'll never be free from this crime until the day I die.

I hear my mother's voice and a child laughing. The child's laugh rings like a bell, announcing my guilt. Soon this child will enter elementary school, and I'll become a school parent. Before June of my sixteenth year, I never imagined I'd be living this way. Not once have I desired this kind of life, yet here I am. What meaning, then, could life possibly hold? I didn't desire such a life for myself, but at the same time, I can't say I didn't choose it.

POEM, 2006

THE SUN was setting. I was making my way down the library steps when I saw a young woman come up the other side, dressed in a beige blouse and yellow skirt. The wide concrete steps were dark gray along the edges, still wet from the previous day's downpour. I glanced at her and then away, and turned my gaze on her once more, unable to help myself. She was extremely thin with a sallow complexion, possibly due to the color of her skirt. As she came closer, I realized she was actually wearing an ombré dress of yellow hues, deepening into a dark yellow at the bottom. The fabric around the shoulders was nearly white, while the hem was closer to the color of mandarin oranges. Yet what caught my attention wasn't her dress, but her face. Or more precisely, her expression. No, you couldn't call it an *expression*, since what wavered over her face was hardly that. In other words, I was struck by the absence of an expression.

It roused a strange feeling in me that was difficult to describe. I'd never seen a mishmash of such bizarre effects on a young woman's face, to the extent that her face itself seemed a riddle. It was both familiar and unfamiliar, one I'd seen long ago yet never seen, and one I wanted to both avoid and scrutinize. She was neither ugly nor dull—maybe she could even be called pretty. In her yellow dress, with the reddish sun spilling out from behind her, she appeared like the bright center of a giant flame. But shadows lurked under that dazzling exterior, just like the steps still wet along the edges.

Sensing my gaze, the girl turned toward me. Her eyes told me she didn't want to be recognized, and she glanced away. I realized then that she knew who I was. Seized by a nameless fear, I nearly turned and bolted to the grassy area beside the steps, but curiosity won out. I walked diagonally down the steps and approached her. She stopped and bowed.

In that instant, a name I'd nearly forgotten burst from my lips.

"Da-on!"

"You recognized me," she said.

Did that mean she was actually Da-on, Hae-on's little sister? Her voice, even the way she spoke, was as unfamiliar as her face.

"Of course."

But to be honest, I still wasn't sure whether the girl standing before me was, in fact, Da-on. If she were to say any second, Sorry, I'm afraid you have the wrong person, I was ready to apologize and continue down the steps.

"You've really—" I started to say, but caught a trace of annoyance that flashed across her face, and said instead, "—lost so much weight."

"You're exactly the same as before, Sanghui eonni," Da-on said, with a faint smile.

The words *before* and *eonni* made me sad, but her smile made me sadder. Da-on had never smiled this way. Even a few years ago, peals of laughter had burst from her open mouth, high and clear, like the bell on a bicycle rolling down a hill. Before I knew what I was doing, I was clutching her arm.

"If you're not busy, let's go have a coffee somewhere."

She flinched. I registered the bony sharpness of her elbow beneath my palm. She had lost a frightening amount of weight.

I WAS in the eleventh grade when my father was discharged from the military. During the several months he was unemployed, the overall mood at home turned glum. My mother, while roasting seaweed or ladling soup, grumbled constantly about how things never worked out for us. When she learned I didn't make it to the top of the class, she clapped her hands and said loud enough for all to hear that I'd done a fine job, it was a good thing after all, since we didn't have money for college anyway. But thanks to the recommendation of his superior, my father eventually found work at a small company, and our family moved from Chungcheong Province to Seoul.

At the end of November, with much anticipation, I transferred to a senior high school in Seoul where girls and boys were taught in separate classes, but I found it hard to make friends, since I'd transferred near the end of the second semester. Our homeroom teacher, who was also the gym teacher, didn't have time to care for a new student like me. He was addicted to playing the stock market, so I learned later.

He scheduled all his classes in the morning and took off as soon as he was finished teaching, not bothering to stick around for lunch, so the class president was usually the one who dismissed us at the end of the day. Everyone, including the class president, seemed to have made a pact never to speak to me. It was almost unbelievable how not one student offered a friendly word. Unable to penetrate the fortress of their relationships, I found myself outside its walls, completely alone.

Soon, I was longing for my old school and my small Chungcheong town. The path snaking down to the school from our home, tin roofs on houses and yards strung with clotheslines sporting colorful clothespins, the blue weathervane that spun dizzily at each gust of wind, the big oak tree in the center of town, and even the bird's nest perched on its branches, like a ball of dark cotton.

I was lonely, but I pretended to be busy with my studies. I ended up actually studying, since it was impossible to only appear as if I were without in fact studying. I'd never experienced such cold weather in my life as I did that winter, walking to and from school. March couldn't come any sooner, when I'd move into my final year of high school and be put in a new class. I thought maybe there would be a chance for me then, a chance to get to know the other students while relationships were still malleable, before they crystallized. So on the last day of my junior year, I was able to look on without emotion, even cheerfully, while the other students made a fuss, bidding each other tearful goodbyes.

In March, on the first day of the school year, I sat in my newly assigned classroom, watching the other girls whisper amongst themselves in groups of twos and threes. They were all building on the foundations they'd already established over the past two years; I was the only one starting from scratch. Things never work out for me, I told myself. Sinking into despair once more, I was glancing around the classroom when I was startled by the sight of a certain girl. She had big almond-shaped eyes that tilted up at the corners ever so slightly and crimson lips like flower petals. She was very pretty, but not in a typical way. How could I describe it? Her beauty was urgent, precarious, like the piercing wail of a speeding ambulance. I could not look away.

But in the next moment, I received an even bigger shock. The pretty girl was scowling at another girl who had been gazing out the window the entire time, who in that instant turned her head, and the loveliness I had glimpsed from her profile bloomed wide, like a parachute bursting open. I felt as if I were going to explode. Her beauty seemed not of this world, a kind you rarely encountered. All of a sudden, the classroom seemed to have transformed into a fictional, perhaps magical, place. I glanced about in a daze, wondering if the class was full of girls as beautiful as these two. I was able to relax only once I'd seen the rest of the students.

That was it. Nothing happened. But after witnessing such astonishing beauty, the other students' faces appeared crude, dreary, even lopsided. I looked at them, feeling both revulsion and relief, and could sense they felt the same as they looked back at me. Fortunately, their hodgepodge of ordinariness pulled me back to reality. We sat in our seats feeling sullen and miserable, like girls who had been passed over, rejected, for lacking some fundamental quality, until the old math teacher, who was also our homeroom teacher, stepped into the classroom. Even Yun Taerim, with her crimson lips and almond eyes, wasn't exactly immune. She was pretty—there was no question about it—but compared to Hae-on's absolute, staggering beauty, she didn't seem all that much different from the rest of us.

Though it's something I would learn later on, Hae-on's younger sister, Da-on, had entered our school that year. Hae-on was already famed among the students, but Da-on also became a subject of conversation soon enough. Not simply because she was Hae-on's sister, but because the two sisters could not have been more different. Hae-on always had a far-off look in her eyes, and she was fair, tall, and slender, with long graceful limbs, while Da-on was short and dumpy, with a plain face. Hae-on was blessed with extraordinary beauty, but her grades were in the mid-low range, whereas Da-on was the freshman rep and had been at the top of her grade. Hae-on was detached and cool, hardly ever speaking or laughing, but Da-on brimmed with passion and curiosity. She was pleasant and savvy in all her dealings, but most of all, she laughed more than anyone.

Their roles were also reversed. Da-on, the younger sister, was the one who looked after Hae-on, as one would after a little sister. She'd stop her big sister on the street before they reached the school gate and then circle her, examining the front and back of her uniform to make sure nothing was out of place. Yet it was Da-on whose white blouse was frequently stained with ink or food, which amused us to no end. Being a freshman, Da-on's classes ended early, but she usually waited outside our classroom until we were done and walked home with Hae-on. As for Hae-on, she usually submitted to Da-on, but there were times she tried to lose her younger sister. Then you could witness the older sister fleeing gracefully down the hall or across the school field with her long lithe limbs, while the younger one raced shrieking after her, like some wild animal. This scene never failed to give both teachers and students a good laugh. That was Da-on's gift. She had a lively, bubbly kind of warmth that could pull Hae-on's devastating, otherworldly, even glacial, beauty into our reality, dissolving it in laughter.

I had the opportunity to get to know Da-on separately, through the school's literary club. I'd picked the club as my extracurricular activity when I'd first transferred. Though I was a latecomer, the enthusiastic young Korean teacher who looked after the club showed me much attention, often praising my poems or asking me to recite them in front of the others. Once students entered their senior year, they could be exempted from extracurricular activities, but she encouraged me to continue with the club, as long as my involvement didn't interfere with my studies. To make my time worthwhile, she offered to pick poems and stories that appeared frequently on college entrance exams for the club readings and discussions.

There was no reason for me to refuse, so I promised to stick with the club, at least for the first semester of my final year.

When I walked into the first club meeting that March, the new students were already there, including Da-on, looking like a country girl with her round rosy cheeks. Though Da-on's poems had a fresh and original quality, they ultimately lacked critical insight and forceful tension—of which she, too, was keenly aware. "Well, isn't that precious?" she'd mutter, mocking herself for trying to sound "cute" when she was hardly that. Or she'd cry that she wanted to wipe out everything she'd ever learned about poetry and hit the reset button, or mumble unintelligibly, smacking herself in the head with her plump fists. Though I related deeply with her sense of frustration, I couldn't help turning away and snickering. The image I'd had back then of the genius poet with restless eyes and a nervous facial twitch, which testified to their sensitive, exquisite mind—an image whose validity I'd never been able to test—could not be further from Da-on's adorable, naive grumbling and bearlike gestures.

Though we'd been together in the same class for nearly half a year, if someone had asked me what Hae-on was like, I would have had nothing to say, other than to mention her terrible beauty that would send a shock both big and small through me each time. Yet about Da-on, whom I saw only once a week at our club meetings for just over an hour, I could have gone on easily enough. About the myriad of expressions that would pass over her face when she talked about poetry, or how she'd practically leaped into my arms when she'd discovered we both liked James Joyce, or her laughter which always told me exactly where she was sitting, without me having to look. Though we were only two years apart, whenever I saw her, I wondered if I'd also been as full of life when I was her age, and I, like an old woman, couldn't help but sink into sadness.

KOREA AND Japan hosted the FIFA World Cup that June. When Korea advanced to the semifinals, even those of us in our senior year couldn't help getting swept up by World Cup fever. Then on June 30, the day of the closing ceremony, I realized with a jolt that June was over. All I could do was tell myself that I would make up for lost time by doing nothing but studying during the summer break. We went back to school on Tuesday, July 2, since the previous day was declared a public holiday. But that day,

Hae-on's seat was empty, and it would remain empty for the rest of the year.

On July 1 in the afternoon, Hae-on's body was discovered in a flowerbed in a park not far from the school. She'd been found with blunt force trauma to the head. The school was turned upside down, engulfed in shock that couldn't compare to the hype of the World Cup.

Recounting and interpreting all the details and rumors about the incident kept us busy until the start of the summer holiday. The teachers weren't able to shut down all the talk, no matter how hard they tried. Students who fancied themselves to be experts drew sketches on the chalkboard or noted the exact timeline of events. Thanks to this education, obtuse students who had believed that *cranial injury* meant a severe injury resembling mashed cranberries soon learned to casually drop crime scene investigation terms into their conversations and even tried to work out who the perpetrator was.

At first the strongest suspect was Shin Jeongjun, but he was soon cleared of all suspicion. The time of Hae-on's death was determined to be between ten p.m. on June 30 and two a.m. on July 1, when I'd been sitting at my desk at home, peering at the calendar and feeling anxious because July was upon us. But Jeongjun's alibis were perfect. Though it was true that around six p.m. on June 30 he'd taken Hae-on for a ride in his new car—or his sister's brand-new car, to be more precise—he'd dropped her off at seven and gone to a high-end Japanese restaurant with friends, who were also the sons of wealthy families. They watched the final World Cup match between Brazil and Germany over dinner and expensive liquor, and then around ten headed to a hotel nightclub famous for attracting pretty girls. He danced and drank all night, making a last stop at the restaurant across the street to have some hangover soup before finally proceeding home. Everyone backed Jeongjun's story: his friends who had been with him, the server at the Japanese restaurant, the nightclub waiter, as well as the owner of the hangover soup restaurant. Soon after the incident, Jeongjun was fined for driving without a license and suspended from school for entering an adult entertainment venue as a minor, but even when his suspension ended, he didn't return to school. They said he'd been withdrawn well before he received his suspension, and was sent to study abroad in America. Then what had been the point of suspending someone who was no longer there? This question, however, failed to become an important issue.

The next-strongest suspect after Shin Jeongjun was Han Manu. Several details from the statement Manu had given about seeing Kim Hae-on in the passenger seat of Shin Jeongjun's car were extremely suspicious and altogether lacked credibility. Some said he'd committed perjury because he was stupid, while others claimed that the shrewd detective had been able to pick out the discrepancies in Manu's carefully crafted story, and still others said Yun Taerim's statement had completely overturned Manu's statement. Rumors circulated. But what became the problem was that Manu lacked a strong alibi.

On June 30, Manu said he had worked at the chicken shop until eleven p.m. and then headed straight home, but the only people who could confirm this detail were his mother and younger sister. However, his mother, who worked the nightshift at a twenty-four-hour hangover soup restaurant, hadn't been home at the time, while his younger sister had been asleep. Though she stated that she'd heard her brother come home in her sleep, the police didn't accept her testimony.

Manu was beaten for refusing to admit to the crime, and threatened and pressured to make a confession. In the end, he was released, since no clear evidence or motive for the murder could be found. But even after his release, detectives continued to show up at his door to question his mother and sister. The students picked sides as to who the real perpetrator was: Shin Jeongjun or Han Manu. At a glance, it seemed more students believed that Han Manu was guilty, probably because the students in this group were generally confident and had no qualms about voicing their opinions. Those who believed that Shin Jeongjun was guilty tended to be cautious and timid. Perhaps because of this, most students were swayed to believe in Jeongjun's innocence.

Han Manu didn't return to school after the summer break. He had dropped out, the school said. No one knew if this decision had been made by Manu or forced on him. Hae-on's sister, Da-on, also transferred schools. People said she had moved far away. The only person involved in the incident who remained was the girl with the crimson lips and almond-shaped eyes: Yun Taerim.

In August when the second semester of my senior year began, silence settled over the entire school. I can't speak for the other classes, but mine was quiet. Of course it didn't stay like that all day. Kids still whispered to each other and fooled around. Then naturally someone would laugh or yell. But unlike before, when laughter and shouts would spread, they withered abruptly. The instant the noise was cut off, an oppressive hush hung heavily over the classroom. We were all seized by the same guilt, and the classroom was as still as the inside of a vacuum. A bizarre gloom and disquiet struck us in the forehead and slipped away.

For a long time whenever I saw the empty spot by the window or walked down the hall by the classroom where the literary club met, I felt as though the space previously occupied by Hae-on and Da-on was now replaced by glass. There were times when I'd been confronted by that void, that invisible presence, and been thrown into confusion. I'm sure the other students have experienced it, too. Gradually, we managed to return to our rightful place, our emotions numbed by the strain and struggle of our looming college entrance exam. We told ourselves: Some of us had to go, that's all. One had an accident, one went abroad, one transferred schools, one dropped out, but we're still here, aren't we? Ah, this is killing us. Nothing's changed. What kind of life is this? Is this living?

And just like that, the incident ended for us. We took the college entrance exam and graduated. Perhaps because she was no longer compared to Hae-on, perhaps because she was in the bloom of youth,

Taerim seemed even more beautiful on graduation day. Just like a vacuum that sucks up everything, she easily commanded all of our attention.

DA-ON AND I headed to the library café. When I asked her what she'd like to drink, she said all she wanted was a glass of water. Still, I got her a lemonade and put it down before her, along with her water, and set my Americano on the table across from her. Now that I was seeing her up close, I realized she was heavily made up.

I engaged her in small talk, asking what someone a few years ahead might typically ask: What was she studying? What career did she intend to take up? I mentioned some classes and clubs that were popular amongst students, as well as a few favorite local spots serving up delicious food. Since I was in my last year, I figured she was entering her second year, but to my surprise, she said she was a freshman. Had she studied an extra year to retake the college entrance exam? No, she'd taken a year off in senior high. I could only nod. Of course I understood. Who could keep attending school as if everything were the same? Her sister had been killed, yet no perpetrator, or any plausible motive, had ever been found. For

Da-on, who'd looked after Hae-on the way a big sister would after a little sister, the pain must have been
indescribable. This is what I was thinking when she
suddenly blurted, "That's when I did it."

Instantly, I knew what she meant. Of course...

"And once I started, I couldn't stop."

I gave another nod. She'd probably taken Hae-
on's picture to the clinic and requested that she be
made to look the same. She'd gone on a diet as well.
My original intention of having an ordinary conversation with Da-on faded. Since she'd brought up her
cosmetic surgery, I decided to follow her cue. "So did
things get better after that?"

"Get better? What do you mean? What could
have gotten better?"

"I just thought...," I said, startled. "Maybe getting it done made you feel better—"

"Ugh! I'm so sick of this!" Da-on cried, with a
shake of her head. She shuddered.

I was stunned. Perhaps it was the effect of the
surgery, but her face contorted unnaturally into a
bizarre, vulgar grimace. A part of me was sad to
see Da-on behave in such an unseemly manner, but
on the other hand, I was confused. I didn't know
whether I should tolerate her rudeness or if I should
get up from my chair and leave. Da-on turned,

shooting a glare at the next table. Three college boys were talking boisterously about the international friendly World Cup match that was to take place between Korea and Senegal in two hours.

I breathed a sigh of relief. Da-on had meant all the soccer talk, not what I'd been saying. Of course I understood. Four years ago, the World Cup and Hae-on's murder had been joined together like a set of Siamese twins, so that if you tugged on one, the other couldn't help but come along. I sipped my coffee in silence. Da-on had her back turned to the boys, sitting rigidly like some yellow crustacean, as if she were determined not to listen to anything they said. Her plastic surgery made her look like her sister, but something was off. In fact, she looked like an older, ruined Hae-on, who had been rejuvenated by force, a cross between the real Hae-on and a ravaged Hae-on. Where had the old Da-on gone?

Da-on glanced at me, her lips set in a smile. No, it was more a scowl. "Why'd you want to come to a place like this?"

I didn't know what to say. What did she mean by *a place like this*? How was I supposed to know a group of college boys would be carrying on about a World Cup game at the library café? Even if we had gone somewhere else, how could I have guaranteed that no one would be talking about the World Cup? Especially on a day when an important match was taking place?

"Did you expect me to tell you everything that's happened once we got here? I bet you were hoping to put on the whole big sister act, patting me on the back with a sympathetic face, telling me to call if I ever wanted to talk."

The corners of Da-on's lips were twisted in a sneer. A wave of dizziness hit me. She was probably right. The kind of scene she described—that's probably what I'd wanted. And that's why I was feeling stunned and confused and ashamed. I had the sudden urge to lash out at Da-on, just as you'd want to kick an injured dog that had growled at you. Though I knew it wasn't right, I wanted to say something to hurt Da-on. I wanted to attack her, because she'd attacked me. Hold on, I told myself, taking a deep breath. After the incident, Da-on must have met many people like me, people who had wanted to offer comfort, yet ultimately judged and resented her when they were confronted with hostility. Yes, I understood. For that reason, I decided to let it go. If I said anything, I'd become like everyone else.

Da-on took a sip of water and picked up her purse. On the rim of the glass was a red imprint of her lipstick. She hadn't touched the lemonade. She stopped as she was about to get to her feet.

"By the way, do you ever talk to Yun Taerim?"

I told her I sometimes saw her at class alumni meet-ups. She took out her phone from her purse.

"You have a number?"

"Who?" I asked, feeling dazed. "My number or Taerim's?"

The corners of her mouth turned up a little. I wondered if that was supposed to be a smile.

"Why would I want her number?" she asked.

I rattled off my number. While she input it into her phone, I waited with my hands clasped neatly together. She looked up. Instead of asking for her number, I asked where she was living now.

"The same place we moved to back then."

I didn't know where that was, but I nodded.

"I live with my mother right now, but I'm going to move out soon. No, not soon. More like some day."

Not knowing if that was a good thing or not, I nodded again.

"But Eonni," Da-on blurted, cocking her head. "Do you still write poetry?"

I felt my face flush at the unexpected question. "No, not anymore," I said, shaking my head.

"I see." She looked at her untouched lemonade. "Lemon...platt."

"Betty Byrne."

Da-on's eyes glittered. In them, I read the same lively energy that the old Da-on used to give off. Did she see something in me, too?

"You remember that, Eonni?"

"I do."

"I hoped you would keep writing your poems."

I was about to ask her why, but ended up saying nothing.

"I used to wish you were my sister instead. I really did. I loved talking to you. Wouldn't it be nice if we could go back to that time..." Da-on took a deep breath, as if she'd lived for a hundred years. "Sorry, I hate myself sometimes. I'll call you. Some day."

With this, she left. Long hair and yellow dress, white purse and white heels. I watched her go, sitting alone and drinking the rest of my coffee that was now cold. The college boys, who had been wrangling over which players should be in the starting lineup against Senegal, got up from their seats. I finished my coffee and started on the lemonade. Because it was growing dark outside, the café seemed much dimmer. All of a sudden, I recalled the lonely winter when I'd first moved to Seoul. The chilly days when not a single soul had talked to me, when I'd eaten alone, studied alone, and walked home alone.

Da-on had asked if I was still writing poetry. Until now, no one had ever asked me that question. After entering teachers' college as my father wished, I'd quit writing. Da-on, once a fan of my poetry, had hoped I'd kept writing. Who else would say something like that to me? Da-on wasn't the only one to have lost something. I'd lost something, too. Maybe I was the more serious case, because she knew exactly what she'd lost, whereas I was trudging through life, ignorant of what I'd lost. I'd sat there scrutinizing her as I listened, nodding my head all too knowingly, as if I understood everything she said. Then when she'd discovered my secret thoughts, I'd wanted to attack her, overcome with anger.

I asked myself: Did I want to go back to that time, too? When I'd been so wild about Joyce that I'd written my poem "Betty Byrne, Maker of Lemon Platt"? If we could actually go back to that time, would I? I didn't know. But I still remember the first lines of that poem.

Today again I burned the platt.
Nothing ever goes right for you, Betty Byrne.

LEMON, 2010

No one—not even my own family—went to my high school or college graduation. Of course, it was only natural my dad and sister didn't attend, but my mother, on the other hand... If I think about it, that too was natural. After all, I didn't go either.

After my sister died, we moved to a new city in Gyeonggi Province. I transferred to the senior high there, an all-girls school this time. Since both Mother and I were falling at a very slow speed, I didn't realize we were falling at first. She went to work at a shop and I went to school. I have no idea how she was managing. As for me, I grew more and more confused, and I hate to admit it, but I began to doubt whether I'd even cared for my sister at all. It was a painful, bitter realization, not because I didn't know if I loved her any longer, but because I didn't know if I ever had. Because this doubt was in the past tense, and therefore something I couldn't change. Because it had been decided forever.

Then everything sped up. We had moved to escape the rumors, to feel my sister's absence less, but our new environment only stimulated our nerves endlessly and called to mind the details of the horrifying incident that had caused us to move. The small void inside my head soon swelled like a balloon, until the whole world dimmed, grew distant, and finally disappeared. All at once my mother and I found ourselves plummeting down a deep well. She quit her job at the shop, and I took a leave of absence from school. We slept for days or were unable to sleep for days. We forgot to eat and didn't have the strength to clean ourselves. Lacking the most basic thought that we needed to climb out of the well, we lay face down in the dank darkness, as if dead, for a long time. Even now, I can't help thinking my passive lethargy in those days was easier, maybe safer. I thought only of my sister, and stayed trapped for days in one murky memory after another, as if nothing else mattered. It must have been the same for Mother. We each had our own guilt to manage.

MY SISTER'S name was originally Hye-eun. It had been my mother who had come up with the name and my dad had gone along with it, but when she suffered from severe postpartum sickness, my sister's birth registration was delayed by a month. During that time, my dad, who was originally from Gyeongsang Province, kept calling my sister *Hae-on* in his provincial accent, to the point that my mom started thinking it wasn't so bad a name, possibly better than Hye-eun. Even if they were to go ahead with the original name, he would keep mispronouncing it anyway, so perhaps it'd be better if they just called her Hae-on from the start. That's how my sister ended up with her name.

If her name hadn't been changed, I might have been Da-eun. I don't know which is better—Da-eun or Da-on. It hardly mattered for me, but in my sister's case, it made a big difference. After she died, Mother began to obsess over the name Hye-eun. She seemed to think my sister's life had gone wrong because of the name change. In the end, my dead sister returned to my mother as Hye-eun. This isn't a metaphor; it's a fact. Ten years after my sister's death, my mother held in her arms a live baby named Hye-eun. This baby was my gift to her.

I'M TOLD my dad adored my sister. I have no doubt she was a beautiful baby, impossible not to love. Since babies are indifferent, selfish creatures who think only of satisfying their needs, perhaps my sister's time as a baby suited her personality more than any other phase in life. I picture her then, when there was no need for her to know language, to know the proper way to form relationships or share her feelings. She must have truly been the brightest creature to ever grace this earth. My dad took her around the whole neighborhood to show her off, and all who laid eyes on her declared they'd never seen a more beautiful baby.

It was a blessing he didn't have to cope with her death. He used to break the first cigarette by accident as he plucked it out from a new pack. Whenever this would happen, he would become red in the face and lose his temper. After living a mundane, dull life, where a trivial incident like this was cause enough for him to become angry, he died.

Before my sister entered elementary school—so when she was six years old and I was four—my dad died in a car accident on a business trip. His colleague had been behind the wheel and my dad had been in the passenger seat, just like my sister, who'd been in the passenger seat of Shin Jeongjun's car. They waited for the left-turn signal at the bottom of a T-intersection, and started to turn left when the signal turned green. At that instant, a truck barreled toward them from the right. Unable to slow down, it rammed into their car, breaking it in two, just like all the cigarettes my dad had snapped by mistake. Because the passenger-side door was badly bent, it took a long time to extricate him from the car. He died before they could pull him out of the wreck. Death by cranial injury, due to a violent blow on the head. His cause of death was the same as my sister's.

OUR RELATIVES murmured that my dad's death had changed my mother, saying she now shrank away from spending money, though she must have gotten quite a bit from the insurance company. She went to work at a friend's shop and left all the house-work to my sister, which was an absurd decision from the start. Our apartment soon became a pigsty. Had our father's death and our mother's subsequent transformation wounded my sister? At least a little, probably. It would have been impossible for her not to have been affected. But I don't think those incidents changed my sister. She was as unyielding as a rock, someone who couldn't be easily changed.

The housework became my responsibility. At the age of five I learned how to run the vacuum cleaner and laundry machine, and at six I rinsed the rice and started the rice cooker and made kimchi stew with tofu and tuna, since I was allowed to use the stove now. Though I spent the entire day with my sister, I had no idea what was going on in her head. It seemed she didn't think about anything. She did nothing and thought nothing. She considered no one and harmed no one. She wasn't interested in anyone nor bothered by anyone. She seemed most content and serene when she was left alone, doing absolutely nothing. The grace and detachment of her gestures— observing someone wordlessly or giving a curt response and then looking away—only enveloped her beauty in dignity. Though this was certainly no ploy to elevate herself, and she was hardly shrewd enough to use such a ploy, she couldn't have found a more suitable method.

Her awareness of the physical body seemed weak and fragile at most. She didn't understand the burden the body carried, and neither did she know the happiness or pains it offered. She treated her own beauty like a pretty pebble she'd happened to find on a beach. Since she was aware that her appearance provided benefits, she sometimes used it to her advantage, but she didn't know its true value. She simply didn't care, just like a child who doesn't see the difference between a pearl and a pebble.

I have no memory of fighting with my sister over treats or toys, but this made me feel sad and anxious rather than happy. I'd always known she and I were fundamentally different. Because she didn't have much of an appetite, I could eat whatever I wanted, as much as I wanted. But when she became hungry, everything changed. She became incapable of empathy, of putting herself in someone else's shoes, and hardly considered another person or the smallest etiquette. In these situations, I had no choice but to wait until she filled her stomach. She seemed like an animal then, or even worse a sociopath, someone who could easily take a piece of bread from a starving child or elderly person. But once satiated, she emerged like an enlightened saint. The sight of her dressed in nothing but a loose nightgown, sitting with her knees bent and spread apart, or lying down and staring off into space, was lovely, but also alarming.

MY MOTHER hit my sister. Not frequently, and not as a consequence of wrongdoing, but in a sudden outburst, like a sneeze. I'm sure my sister's apathy at home or neglect of her studies was partly to blame, but the main reason had to do with her carelessness: she often went around without any underwear.

Once, my mother raised her hand to strike my sister when she'd gone to and from middle school without any underwear, let alone a bra. Then all of a sudden, my mother dropped her hand and peered into my sister's face instead, as if seeing her for the first time. I don't know what she saw in the lovely face that gazed brightly up at her. She trembled and gave a series of solemn nods. I read in my mother's expression infinite hope and pride and the burden of responsibility and resolve; she looked like someone who held a rare precious object in her hand.

After that incident, my sister's underclothes became my responsibility, just like the housework.

Before stepping out of the house, I stood her before me and circled her, checking her uniform to make sure she hadn't forgotten anything. When I entered senior high, I felt better only after I'd checked her once more in front of the school gate, since my sister was a senior—a woman, practically. After all, it would be awful if a woman forgot to wear a bra and underwear.

ALL THROUGHOUT that summer, I suffered from terrible acne and spent my days unintentionally looking like the mascot of the Korean soccer team's fan club—a Red Devil in every sense of the word. I even saw a dermatologist, but the acne didn't clear. I resorted to joking that I'd turned my face red on purpose to match my World Cup shirt.

The day after the World Cup ended was declared a national holiday. When the phone rang that evening, I was in the bathroom, folding the wings of a sanitary napkin onto the backside of my underwear. I waited for the phone to stop ringing, but when it continued, I tugged up my underwear and hobbled out of the bathroom, doubled over with menstrual cramps. When the caller asked to speak to my sister's guardian, I told him the number of the shop where my mother worked. I headed back to the bathroom, and pulled down my underwear once more. Out of breath, I was about to readjust the pad when I glanced up and caught my reflection in the mirror: my hideous red face, covered with pus-filled pimples, and the hairy black patch between my legs, sticky with blood. Now here was the real Red Devil, I thought. Why was I so ugly? If only I could have been my sister...When I glanced down and saw the pad stained with blood, I had trouble breathing all of a sudden. Who had that been on the phone just now? Why had he wanted to speak to my sister's guardian?

A moment later, Mother called and told me to check if my sister was home. I looked in my sister's room, my mother's, and even mine, but she wasn't there. Mother, with her voice shaking, ordered me not to go anywhere, to lock the door and stay put.

My mother came home late that night, drenched with rain. I hadn't realized it was raining outside. I went and got a rag right away. She flopped down on the living room floor and cried, "Hye-eun's dead!"

I still can't forget her voice from that day, the way she'd said *Hye-eun* instead of *Hae-on*.

I hear her voice right now. I hear her calling, Hye-eun, Hye-eun. Oh, there you are, my little lamb! There you are.

LOOKING BACK now, what strikes me as strange is that neither my mother nor I noticed my sister hadn't come home the night before.

That evening, I'd believed my sister was home. Because she wasn't interested in things like the World Cup, I watched the final match between Brazil and Germany alone and made myself some instant noodles, which I ate, while watching the closing ceremony. My mother, who returned from the shop late, didn't think it strange that the front door was unlocked, and neglected to gather her daughters to tell them to be more careful.

I still don't know why my sister left our apartment earlier that day. She never went for walks, and she didn't step out to buy something, since she didn't take her wallet with her. But what I really can't understand is why she'd been in Shin Jeongjun's car. She wasn't one to go along with something she didn't want to do. The laundromat lady confirmed she hadn't been forced. So why had she gotten into Shin Jeongjun's car in front of the laundromat? Where had she been heading? And where had she gone after she climbed out of his car, at around seven p.m.? Since she wasn't carrying

any money, she couldn't have taken the bus or subway to the park, five bus stops away. Then did she
walk all the way there, where her body was eventually discovered? Whom did she meet there? Who
killed her?

THE PERIOD of being stuck in a deep well finally
came to an end. One day I observed my mother picking up objects and studying them, and then either
moving them elsewhere or placing them inside something. I had to watch for a while before I realized
she was cleaning. In order to help, I picked up the
objects around me and studied them as well. I held
a long bottle with a curved neck and blue cap for a
long time. Where was it supposed to go? I seemed to
know and not know. What was inside—something
cool or sticky? Only when I caught a whiff of men-
thol did I realize it was supposed to go in the first aid
box marked with a red cross. I hadn't been sure if
it was liquid glue or roll-on muscle relaxant. In this
way, my mother and I returned to reality. Mother
went back to work at her friend's shop and I planned
to go back to school as soon as the summer break
was over. Back then, I'd thought that we'd finally

escaped. Survived. But I was wrong. We hadn't re-turned at all.

My MOTHER went to Family Court to try to get my sister's name changed. When she said that she wanted to change her daughter's name, she was given an application form and told about the other documents she needed to submit. After returning home, she printed my sister's name neatly on the name change form, as well as her own name, ad-dress, and other personal information, since she was my sister's guardian. As for the reason for the name change, she explained that her daughter's name was originally supposed to be Kim Hye-eun, but it had been registered incorrectly, and she wanted to get it fixed; better late than never.

When she went back to Family Court to submit her application, the employee asked for the supple-mental documents. Mother responded by saying she hadn't been able to get the Family Relation Certificate because her daughter had died. Unable to hide her surprise, the employee asked if she was trying to obtain a name change for the deceased. Serenely, my mother replied that was correct, to which the employee said changing the name of the deceased was not possible. My mother refused to give up. What difference was there between changing the name of someone who was alive, as opposed to someone who was not? she asked. And what was so difficult about complying with her request? The employee said it wasn't that the request was too difficult, but it simply was not possible. And even if the name change were granted, where would she need to register this new name? What good would a name change do, since the deceased cannot belong to associations and has no need to fill out any documents? Still, my mother said none of this mattered; all she wanted was to change my sister's name. "I'm afraid I can't do that," the employee said, shaking her head, face drained of all color. "It isn't possible to change the name of the deceased." With that, she returned my mother's thousand-won processing fee on a small rectangular tray. Mother gazed blankly at the paper bill and mumbled, "My daughter died, but you can't do this one small thing?" And like a child who was the only one denied sweets, she picked up her money and left, fighting back tears.

After that, she took it upon herself to change my sister's name. She seemed determined to perform this task on her own. She pulled out all of my

sister's textbooks, references, notebooks, and plan-
ners and corrected the name on each cover. She took
out every one of my sister's photos from our albums
and printed my sister's new name on the back of
each picture. She even took out the housekeeping
books she'd started to use after my dad passed away,
whited out my sister's name next to any expense
attributed to her, and printed her new name. Hae-
on's gym clothes, Hae-on's running shoes, Hae-on's
stationery—they all became Hye-eun's belongings.

"Your sister *Hye*-eun," she would say, stressing
the first part of her name. But sometimes she would
overdo it and the syllable ended up sounding more
like *hwe* or *sye*. As I listened to her, I didn't think
it was my mother who was being unreasonable. I
blamed the employee. She'd caused all this trouble
by refusing my mother's request. What good would a
name change do? she'd asked. Who was she to worry
about that? What right did she have? If she'd simply
done as my mother wished, all this could have been
avoided.

ONCE WHEN I woke up, I found my mother sitting
by my side, peering intently at me, her face set in a
grimace. I didn't know how long she'd been in that

position. Though I was awake now, she continued to stare at me, with no change in her look. She was wearing the kind of expression you might see on someone whose hangnail had torn off. I realized she was searching not for me but another. She was longing for another face, as if wondering, Where is the face I loved? Why is this face here instead?

If there was an opposite of how my mother's eyes had once blazed with pride and hope as she gazed at my sister, it was how she gazed at me in that moment. I realized then that we hadn't returned to reality. In fact, we would never return, unless we adjusted our course drastically. What awaited us was a lifetime of twitches and convulsions, of endlessly performing and aborting and repeating actions, just as some patients with anxiety disorders shake and blink and are unable to sit still, out of fear of losing themselves.

Powerless to change herself, my mother had resorted to changing my sister's name. Similarly, because I couldn't change a thing about my sister, I decided to change myself. Even if my mother had tried to stop me, I would have still gone ahead, but she didn't try. If anything, she encouraged it, offering me the money for the surgery, despite having been rather stingy all her life. I inquired at different clinics. I started with my eyes and lips, followed by my forehead and nose. In the end, I received three sessions of facial contouring surgery on my cheekbones, chin, and lower jaw. The pain was like a drug. While the splint was taped over my nose, while tears ran down my swollen cheeks, I was finally at peace, just as my sister had once been.

TWO AND a half years after my sister's death, I finally worked up the courage to go to the park. I took the subway from the new city to the station near our old apartment, and then got on the local bus. The park wasn't very big. If you took the narrow trail that veered left off the main path, you came to a secluded spot with a wooden bench. To the left of the bench was a metal box the size of a suitcase— probably an electrical box—and behind that stood a tall green wire fence. The dried grass angled down toward the fence, steep enough to send a ball rolling quickly down the slope. I stood on this patch of grass between the bench and fence. It was here that my sister's body had been discovered.

On this clear winter day, the bare trees made the area seem open and exposed, but everything would have looked very different in late June. The trees would have been full of leaves, and the ground green with grass. On top of that, the ground sloped so steeply away that a body would have been difficult to spot, unless in broad daylight. My sister had been discovered around two in the afternoon by an elderly couple who had come out for a stroll. Though her underclothes were missing, the autopsy didn't reveal any traces of rape or sexual assault.

I often went to the park after that and sat on the bench for a long time before returning home. In both my dreams and waking life, I frequently found myself there. My sister is sitting on the bench, wearing a sleeveless yellow cotton dress. She's just like a woodland fairy, with her long black hair loose over her shoulders and her gaze fixed on some distant point, a dreamy look in her eyes. But no, she isn't gazing at anything. She doesn't see anything, actually. All of a sudden, a hand appears from the darkness behind her. The hand is clutching something like a rock, and with it, strikes my sister's head. Several times, the hand comes down on her head. Blood splatters on her yellow dress. She falls over. The hand drags her into the shadows, and my sister, like a flower withering, becomes swallowed up by the darkness. Where am I in this moment? Where am I watching from? Whether asleep or awake, I don't know where I am.

Once I got an eerie feeling and came to with a start. It had begun to rain at some point and I found myself sitting on the bench in the park, soaked to the skin. Then there were times when I believed I was in the park, but I was actually at home. Just as my sister once had, I was sitting on the sofa with my knees spread out to the sides. On the coffee table were pens, a notepad, and the TV remote controller. I felt a stare on me, but no one was there. No, something was there. A roll of toilet paper sitting on the left side of the table—the hole seemed to be glaring at me. It seemed to avoid my gaze if I looked at it head-on, but when I turned away, I felt its one-eyed stare on the left side of my chin, still swollen from surgery. I couldn't understand the reason for that stare, but I soon realized it was mocking me. I jumped to my feet and hurled the toilet paper on the floor and stepped on it. The roll flattened and the eye closed at last. It died. I'd killed it. It was my sister, and it was also me. We'd both died. I was no longer Da-on. Maybe I was Chae-on or Ta-on someone or other, but I wasn't Da-on, not on the outside, not on the inside. Holding the flattened roll, I sank to the floor and cried. I cried, not knowing who I was supposed to become. I tore off some toilet paper and wiped my tears. Like those who had no idea their youth was gone, I'd lost myself without realizing it.

NO MATTER where I was, I could always feel a stare on my face. Sometimes, it was a person staring, but more often than not, it turned out to be an object. Objects watched me constantly. There was no escape. My entire body tensed, trying to endure these stares, until different parts of my body would strain, even when I was alone. Completely tense, I'd finally explode, unable to bear it any longer, and would flatten objects, crush them underfoot, perhaps hurl them. These objects had to be soft, shatterproof, since I could no longer bear the sound of something breaking or being smashed to pieces. Merely imagining these noises was enough for terror to take hold. I didn't just hear these noises—I saw them with my eyes. If things crashed together and shattered, my eyes grew wide and began to twitch. Shrieks erupted, turning everything before me into a fiery hell, and while this vision raged, hot tears flowed down my face like blood.

———

THE DAY before my college graduation, I started running a fever around noon. My throat hurt and my face was hot. My mother hadn't returned from the shop yet. I took some medicine from the first aid box and gargled with a warm salt solution. I saw my flushed face in the mirror, the redness along the incision sites.

I woke in the middle of the night and took some more medicine. After sleeping for a long time, I finally got up late in the afternoon. My mother had already left for work. The ceremony would have been over by now. I pulled out two eggs from the refrigerator and put them in a pot of water. While I waited for the eggs to boil, I sat on the sofa and hallucinated I was in the park again. My sister, sitting on the bench, as lovely as a yellow freesia. A loud thud. Blood-soaked hair. Coarse pubic hair clumped with menstrual blood. Yellow and red flowers sucked up by darkness. A face flushed red. These images overlapped and splintered and scattered. I heard the pot boiling over.

I turned off the stove and placed the eggs in cold water. Since I couldn't tap the egg to break the shell, I peeled it by rolling it gently on the table. The late afternoon sun that spilled in through the living room window revealed a layer of dust on the table. I took a bite, and tasted the soft white and jammy yolk. I glanced down. The yolk glistened in the light. I couldn't help thinking how lovely it looked.

For a very long time, I hadn't thought anything was lovely. I recalled all of a sudden how I had asked Sanghui eonni if she was still writing poetry when I'd run into her a few years ago. Lemon... The brilliant yellow of the yolk was making me want to write poetry once more. For now, as long as I was gazing at the yolk nestled next to the white, I didn't feel lonely. I felt no pain. I was at peace, like a baby in a cradle. I felt my consciousness open its eyes and stretch lazily, as if waking from a winter's sleep. *Ha-an-man-u-u-u...*

I decided to pay him a visit. No, the thought came like a revelation. A lump of energy, dull and sluggish until now, was quickening, growing hot. Finally, the time to act had come. I needed to begin with him. I wasn't sure, but that much I knew. In my mind, it was his hand that came out of the darkness. That night between 11:30 p.m. and midnight, on his way home after work, he would have seen my sister in the park and killed her for reasons I don't know. It wouldn't have required too much time to bash her in the head, and then move her body to the bottom of the grassy slope. He would have hurried home and announced his arrival loudly, so that his younger sister, asleep until then, would confirm his alibi later on, even though she hadn't checked the exact time he'd returned. But what doesn't make sense is why he had risked almost everything by saying she'd been dressed in shorts and a tank top. Instead of confirming his innocence, it had only seemed as if he were trying to cover up his guilt.

I rolled the second egg on the table, peeled it, and took a bite. I needed to see him. I needed to know how he was getting on, so that I could figure out who I was supposed to become, how I was supposed to live. I needed to see him if I wanted to go on. These thoughts swept over me and I felt a strange surge of excitement. It meant I needed to leave my mother. I needed to move out. If she were left all alone . . . could she survive without me? Maybe if just for a little while—no, don't think about that now. Not now.

At last a door that had been shut for a long time was opening, and radiant light came flooding in. And so began the revenge of the yellow angel. Lemon, I muttered. Like a chant of revenge, I muttered: Lemon, lemon, lemon.

ROPE, 2010

•

HELLO? IS this the 24/7 Lifeline? I have an appointment to speak to a counselor right now.

You need to verify my information? Sure, my ID is *Christ*. That's C-H-R-I-S-T, *Christ*, as in Jesus Christ. I'm twenty-six years old, and I'm single.

Is there anything else you need? You'll connect me to a counselor now? Yes, I'll hold.

HELLO, MY ID is *Christ*. Yes, this is my first time calling. I actually hesitated a lot about putting in this request. You see, I need help—desperately. It's a very long and painful story, but I just can't go on like this anymore. I really need to talk to someone. I can't sleep at night, and I'm starting to see and hear things. I feel like I'm going to lose my mind.

But I wanted to check something first. Is our conversation being recorded? Oh, it is? Would it be possible to not record our session? I see...It's your policy to record all counseling sessions...Then can you promise that what I'm about to say here—everything that gets recorded—will be confidential? Oh, it's safe then...And it'll all be deleted after a certain period? What a relief. But what if it's needed for an investigation? Or the government, like the police, requests it? Forget confidentiality then—couldn't the entire recording be used as evidence? That rarely happens? Even so, it's a patient's statement and—what did you say? A patient with mental illness, even if they confess to a crime, can't be held responsible? That's the law? If that's true...I guess I don't have a problem.

Pardon me? What problem do I mean? Sorry, I can't really hear you.

Doctor, are you drinking something right now? You're having coffee? What kind? Cuban? I see. Because of my heartburn, I had to quit coffee more than a year ago. I got rid of everything then. I got rid of my Belgian grinder, too, which I'd absolutely adored. I didn't give it to anyone—I just threw it out. It seemed to be the only way I'd be able to quit coffee. But I really miss it. Especially the smell. A hot, strong cup of coffee...Oh, what I would do for just one sip...

Can I ask you another question, Doctor? What happens if I talk about someone else, about a crime that they committed? Does that mean the statement— you called it a *statement*, didn't you—won't be accepted or considered valid, since it's given by someone who's mentally unstable? No, I understand what you mean...yes, of course it depends on the situation. After all, aren't laws ambiguous? I know a little about how they work, since I majored in poli sci— you know, political science. If there's no ambiguity or flexibility in law, why would we need politics or diplomacy? People say there is but one law, that everyone's equal before the law, but they have no clue. Nope, they sure don't. The law isn't some machine, and people who deal with laws aren't machines, so how could it be applied equally every single time? I believe the law is divine. We can't expect powerless humans like us to understand the ways of God! Maybe the law is actually an all-knowing, mighty being. Or a force you can't measure or fight or avoid! Or maybe it's a will...Doctor, do you believe in Jesus by any chance? Even if you're nonpracticing, I thought maybe you go to church. Is that right? You see, I'm a pretty devout Christian. That's why I chose *Christ* as my ID.

Oh, I've really gone off on a tangent, haven't I? Sorry about that. I guess I brought up an extreme example like crime, because I'm about to tell you something deeply personal...You see, all my life, I've never had anything to do with crime or violence. I don't know people from that world, thank God. I know I'm lucky. Sometimes, though, I can't help thinking it's a shame. You know how in movies there's something quite attractive about violent rebellions? About things like resistance and revolutionary forces? Do you think that's ludicrous? I guess I'm still like a child, dreaming of adventure...Ah, why do I keep rambling like this...

All right, shall I start then? I'm getting married soon, but I have a serious problem. The man I'm marrying was my boyfriend from high school—we went to the same school—but in his senior year, he went to the U.S. to study and just moved back to Korea this spring. As soon as he got back, he tracked me down, and without any warning, asked me to marry him—boy, was I shocked! When I didn't say yes right away, he asked me if I didn't think it was a decent arrangement. Yes, that's the word he used—*arrangement*. Of course, he was joking. He said it as a joke. He's always joking around.

What does he do for a living? He's an accountant at a big important firm. His father worked there for a long time, too. He comes from a family of accountants. His mother and I went to the same college, and his family's also Christian. I used to attend another church, but she recommended that I move to theirs, so I did. One of our church members used to be a justice in the Supreme Court, and many of them are in the legal profession. We also have members of the National Assembly, cabinet ministers, university professors, and artists. Many celebrities attend, too. To be honest, I couldn't help being disappointed by some of them when I saw them in person. They were short and small, and reminded me of puppets in a way. They looked so different in person! My fiancé's mother said the same thing. She said I'm better-looking than most actresses. I wonder why she'd say something like that to me?

Oh, my problem? The thing is, I'm a little worried about marrying him because, first of all, we're still young and ... I'm scared he's going to control me. Do you know what I mean? I'm scared he'll want to maybe tie and lock me up. I'm sure you've heard of men like that. Men who try to control the women they love. Of course, deep down I don't believe he'd be that immature. I mean, he's been through hell himself in the past. But couldn't that make him crueler? Since he's been through something so horrible, he might think nothing of doing something worse, you know? Maybe he wouldn't even blink an eye...

What happened in the past? I'd rather not discuss it now. I mean, it wasn't that big of a deal. Did I say it was horrible? Maybe for him. I guess it was horrible, if you think about it. The way he went on about how there's no knowing who suffered more, how he had it the worst... God, he was so scared then. Scared out of his mind. Still, didn't he run off to America and get off scot-free?

Pardon me? What did you say, Doctor? What am I doing right now? Talking to you, of course. You want to know what's in my hand? Oh, just a hair tie. You know, something to tie your hair with. It's green and sparkly. I'm just wrapping it around my hand and then unwrapping it. Do I do this often? Not often, maybe sometimes. Actually, maybe often. I'm not really sure. Why? Is this bad? It's a little complicated? Yes, please tell me next time. Doctor, you sure seem observant. Nothing gets past you, does it? I don't know why, but I feel like I can trust you. I wish I could tell you everything.

All right, I'll talk about what happened. I want to. At least briefly. Actually, I'll try to be as detailed as possible. I don't think I'd be able to talk about anything else if I leave out what happened. So going back to the very beginning... He and I used to be in a serious relationship. Everyone thought we were perfect for each other. Everyone? I mean... our friends, of course. His friends, my friends—they all thought so. Everyone envied us. We really did share a perfect, innocent love. If we'd been able to go on like that, I know we could have been happier than anyone out there... But all of a sudden, she got in the way. Another girl. She came in between us and I... I didn't know what to do. I had no idea he'd change that fast. I couldn't believe it. Did he love her? Did he... love... her?

No! No! He didn't love her! Of course not! It wasn't love. The only thing she had going for her was her looks. She was that kind of girl. Stuck-up, got the worst grades in school—you won't believe how dumb she was. An airhead like that got between us and he... he... it was just for fun... you know how guys get. Maybe he was trying to make me jealous.

I swear he never loved her. Not for a second. That's right, all he wanted was to have a little fun, the way you'd play around with a toy. But when things didn't go the way he wanted, he got frustrated. He just can't stand not getting his way, so that's probably why he wanted to get rid of her.

Pardon? What did you say? Me? Why? Why would I do that to her...? I was talking about him, not me. He must have gotten so frustrated he wanted to kill her. No, of course, he didn't want to kill her for real! He probably just wanted to give her a little scare. Why? I'm not sure. Can you believe she tried to seduce him by wearing nothing under her dress—I mean, she met him not just without a bra, but without any underwear! So is that why he killed her? Of course not, Doctor, how can you say such a thing? He said he didn't kill her. I mean, he didn't kill her! He really didn't.

It's the truth. He couldn't even try anything with her. All he wanted was to teach her a lesson, but she went completely berserk like a crazy cat and killed herself... Why? What do you mean why? Because... she was ashamed... Because she'd tried to seduce him, but failed... That's probably why she committed suicide. Yes, this really happened. She hit

78

her head against the wall until … cranial injury … she died of a cranial injury. Just thinking about it gives me the creeps … God … it's so horrible … How could an eighteen-year-old girl do that … bash her head against the bathroom wall … bash her head in until the marble cracked … until she died … just because she was tied up … how could she do something so awful … ahhh … I'm scared … she went crazy … she completely lost it …

PARDON ME? What did you say, Doctor? What do you mean was she tied up? Who? That girl? Why would she be tied up? No, I never said anything like that. You must have heard wrong. I didn't say that. Really! I never said anything.

Why in the world would I say that? I told you I didn't! What? A rope? What rope? What are you talking about? She wasn't tied up, why are you going on about a rope? Are you crazy? You're accusing me of tying her up? I had nothing to do with it! You better stop treating me like this! What's the matter with everyone?

———

HELLO? HELLO?

Doctor? Are you still there? Did you hang up?

No! I didn't finish my story! I didn't do anything wrong. I didn't see her in shorts! I said I didn't, because I didn't see her in them—what's wrong with that? I swear to God, all I did was tell the truth. I didn't make anyone suffer. That guy—that nice dumb guy...what was his name? Ha-an man-u-u...Han Man...u. That's right, Han Manu! He was released right away, so what's the problem? I never wanted her dead. I swear. I've never seen anyone more beautiful. But why is she so scary in my dreams? Ahhh...I'm so scared. Isn't anyone there?

Hmph!

What did you say? An arrangement?

How dare he call it an arrangement? How dare he—that asshole! What does he take me for? Doesn't he realize what would have happened to him if it hadn't been for me? Chickenshit pervert! Evil demon! He made an innocent angel die! Murderer!

Ah, Jesus! Loving Jesus!

Please forgive that asshole...No, don't forgive him...I pour out my heart before you with tears, loving Jesus, won't you help me...You know I'm blameless, please help me find a way...Would your strong hand lead me out of the valley of the shadow of death...I ask for your wisdom...Please give me your spirit of discernment...

Ah...is no one there? I'm scared...Please...I'm so scared...

KNEES, 2010

•

WHEN I climbed to the top of the hill, I saw a commercial building with a church on the second floor. A cross adorned each second-story window. On the ground floor at the left of the building was a small shoe repair shop, the word *shoe* written vertically on one sliding door and *repair* on the other. I rounded the corner, marveling over the fact that shoe repair shops still existed, when I came across a sign that read WE BUY GOLD TEETH AND GOLD SPOONS. It would have been more appropriate if the writing had been in gold or yellow, but it was in red ink. To draw attention no doubt. I couldn't help picturing a bloody spoon going into a bloody mouth.

On a small plot of remnant land behind the building stood two narrow five-story apartment houses. He lived in the mid-rise on the right, in Suite 301 of Building A. That's what the chicken shop owner had said. He not only remembered him, but seemed to think highly of him. "Didn't look it, but he worked real hard. Sure was a fine boy and fine worker. With a good head on his shoulders, too. A worker like that's hard to come by."

I walked up the steps and rang the bell to 301. I heard a man's voice call, "Who is it?"

"Is this the residence of Han Manu?"

Soon after, the door opened. I could tell at once he wasn't doing too well. He'd lost weight and his hair had thinned, making him look old for his age, but more than anything, he had a pair of crutches wedged under his arms.

"Sorry, but...do I know you?"

He didn't know who I was. Though I'd hardly expected him to recognize me right away, I never imagined he'd be so calm. My hair was down, but most importantly, I had on a sleeveless yellow dress with sandals.

"Can I help you?"

I ran my hand through my hair and blurted, "Kim Hae-on!"

"Kim Hae-on?"

A few seconds later, he flinched and peered closely at me.

"I'm her little sister, Kim Da-on."

"Kim Da-on?"

"I need to talk to you about something. Can I come in?"

As soon as I stepped forward, he took a step back. His left pant leg looked strangely slack. I removed my sandals and went inside. The television was turned on in the cramped living room to my right, and a worn sofa sat opposite the screen. Instead of cushions, a blanket was spread on the sofa, with a depression in the middle, as if he'd been sitting there until a moment ago. The kitchen was on the left, with a small table pushed up against the wall, three chairs, and a folded wheelchair. No one else seemed to be home.

I pulled out a chair and sat down. He pressed a button on the remote control to turn off the television and stood across from me, propping his crutches against the wall. I saw the kitchen sink behind him and the small window above. All of a sudden, I recalled what the detective had said, about his habit of dragging his feet. I didn't know whether his injured leg was still healing or if his leg was beyond recovery so that he'd never be able to drag his feet again, but even if that were the case, I didn't think the punishment was enough.

"Did you get into an accident?"

"There was no accident," he mumbled.

"Then what's wrong with your leg?"

"I had to get surgery."

"What kind of surgery?"

"I got sick."

"Did you have to amputate?"

He hung his head in silence, appearing tired and sad. I wanted to stir up my hatred, to spit cruel and bitter words at him, so that I wouldn't feel the least bit sorry for him.

"You're being punished!"

"It's because I got sick," he mumbled. "That's why the military gave me a disability discharge."

The unfamiliar term *disability discharge* threw me into confusion for a moment, but I cried, "What I'm saying is, your illness isn't going to stop there!"

With a sigh, he bowed his head and waited meekly, as if wishing whatever was coming next would end quickly. But I wasn't ready to let him off the hook so easily.

"Look," I said, pointing to my yellow dress. "Does this remind you of anything?"

He glanced at my clothes.

"You saw something like this that night, didn't you? You must have seen the dress my sister was wearing."

He said nothing.

"Don't tell me you're still planning to insist she was wearing shorts and a tank top. When you knew all along she was wearing a dress!"

I registered the shock in his small eyes. "She wasn't wearing shorts? Why are you saying she wasn't?"

Just as the detective must have wanted to, I wanted to strike his ugly face for the way he went on about the shorts.

"Did you think you'd be safe if you stuck to your little story? How could you see her in shorts when she wasn't even wearing them? That's why it's you. That's why it has to be you. I'm not trying to get you arrested. What can I do anyway? It's all over now. I just want to know who killed her and why, that's all. It was you, wasn't it? You killed my sister, didn't you?"

"You probably won't believe me," he mumbled at last, "but I didn't see anything that day. Hae—" He broke off, as if he were afraid to put my sister's name on his lips. "I didn't even see her sitting in the passenger seat. I was looking straight ahead, because the light was going to change any second. Taerim was the one who told me everything."

"You liar! Taerim said she saw my sister in the car, but couldn't tell what she was wearing on the bottom. And the detective said it was only natural Taerim couldn't see."

"He's right. I mean, the detective's probably right."

"What?"

"Taerim probably couldn't see. But she said your sister was wearing shorts. She said it while sitting right behind me."

He grinned. All of a sudden, my skin broke out in goosebumps. The murderer was actually grinning . . .

"Right then, the light changed. As I was starting the scooter, Taerim held on to me and said, 'She's wearing a tank top with shorts.' That's what she said. I remember it so clearly."

He gave another grin. I couldn't understand why he kept grinning.

"But that doesn't make sense! Why would she say that when she couldn't see?"

"I thought it was strange, too, so I asked her how she could tell. Then she said, 'You idiot. Look how she's sitting with her knees spread apart like that, so of course she's wearing shorts.' That's what she said."

All at once, my head emptied. I turned and glared at the pill bottles and medicine packets piled at the edge of the table against the wall. Her knees! He'd said how she'd been sitting with her knees spread apart. I knew that posture better than anyone. Hardly caring whether she was in a skirt or dress, my sister would put her feet on the sofa and let her knees flop to the sides, revealing her crotch. It had horrified both me and my mother to no end. If she'd been sitting the same way in the car as she'd sat on the sofa at home, anyone who saw her through the car window would have assumed she was wearing shorts. Taerim would have thought so, too.

He said something else, but I couldn't hear. When I finally roused myself, he was mumbling, as if talking to himself.

"I really wanted to leave Taerim out of it. But the detective kept asking me about Jeongjun's car, if I was positive I saw Hae—um, your sister in the passenger seat. That's why I repeated what Taerim had told me, about her hair being down and what she was wearing. But he kept saying I was wrong and told me to think really hard, because I must have seen wrong. I don't think Shin Jeongjun mentioned he'd given Hae—uh, her a ride. Well, not at first. Then when the detective kept grilling me about her shorts, if I actually saw her in them, I had to bring Taerim up. But I wish I'd never said anything."

"Why didn't you mention my sister's knees?" I asked. "Why didn't you say you didn't see anything, that you only repeated what Taerim told you? That she was just assuming, too? Why didn't you say any of this?"

"I don't know. I just assumed Taerim would tell him."

"Didn't you know she said nothing about my sister's knees or the shorts?"

"Yeah, the detective told me."

"Then why didn't you say anything?"

"Because Taerim didn't." He smiled once more. "I just assumed there was a reason why. Then later, I thought maybe it was a girl thing."

"A girl thing?"

"I don't know. Taerim must have had a reason, right? So I didn't say anything either. She was having a really hard time, you know. The detective kept asking if she'd actually seen Hae—uh, her in Jeongjun's car. He left her alone only after she told him the color of the tank top."

"So...did you meet with Taerim?"

He didn't answer for a while. "Yeah, I did...," he said at last. Slowly, he continued, "Just once. She came to the chicken shop. I've never told anyone this—not even the detective..."

He peered into my eyes, as if he were conspiring with me. "When I came out after my shift, Taerim said she'd waited over half an hour for me."

His face brightened noticeably. His eyes became clearer and the lines on his face seemed to fade.

"That's when she told me it's hard for girls to talk about stuff like that, you know, how she was sitting with her knees spread. Taerim asked me not to say anything. I realized then it must be a girl thing."

Taerim, Taerim, Taerim...Every time he talked about her, the pinched look left his face and he no longer resembled a pickle. Instead, his face appeared brighter, more alert; he seemed more like a canary melon. Then I recalled my sister's smooth, round knees that had been like baby melons. He pointed at my clothes and said, "But are you saying she was wearing a dress that day, not shorts?"

I didn't answer him. I had no desire to confirm she'd been sitting that way in a dress. He didn't pry. When I stood up from the chair, he looked at me as if surprised. It seemed he'd been preparing himself for a long ordeal.

I left his apartment. The whole time as I was walking down the steps, my legs shook. My sister's knees... It was something I'd never imagined. She was quite cautious when she was wearing her school uniform, but not in anything else. She was hardly aware of it. It was one of the reasons why she usually stayed home. That day my sister had been in a loose sleeveless yellow dress she wore around the house and a pair of flip-flops. She'd been wearing nothing underneath. Shin Jeongjun would have seen. My sister, who had sat with her knees flung apart without any underwear... He would have seen everything. I squeezed my eyes shut. I clenched my teeth so that I wouldn't scream. I understood how my mother had felt, as she'd raised her hand impulsively to slap my sister.

I WENT to see him many times after that. I asked what I had already asked, and heard what I had already heard. In the end, I'd memorized nearly everything he'd told me so that if he faltered or said something a little different, I'd prompt or even correct him. Sometimes we sat across from each other without saying a word. There was nothing new to learn, yet I kept visiting him. I'd believed that if I tracked him down and heard what he had to say, everything would be resolved at last, but I still hadn't figured out how I was supposed to live.

On my fifth visit, he let me in without a fight, just as he always did. As soon as I stepped through the front door, I heard a girl's cheerful voice call out, "Who's that?"

It was his younger sister. Even though I knew she was the only one who had confirmed his alibi, it felt strange to think he had a sister. A face popped out from the kitchen. With her round face and big eyes with double eyelids, she looked nothing like him. Just as I'd looked nothing like my sister. She shot him a glance, but seemed to figure out who I was right away.

"Why do you keep coming here?"

I didn't know what to say.

"Didn't you hear me? Why are you here?"

"To get my shoes fixed..."

"Your shoes?" she asked, her eyes widening. "What are you talking about?"

"There's a shoe repair shop here..."

"Oh, that shop. But why do you have to come to our place?"

"I don't want to pick a fight. I just want to talk."

When I took off my shoes and tried to step inside, she stood in front of me, blocking my way. She was very short. So short that I could see the top of her head.

"About what? My brother said he's told you everything."

"I didn't come to talk about that. It's about something else."

"Sure, that's what they all said. They'd come see me and my mother, acting like they wanted to ask us about something else, but they wouldn't believe anything we told them. Then later on, they'd pick every little thing apart. It was ridiculous."

"I'm not the police."

"Still, you came here to do some investigating of your own, didn't you? I bet you're hoping to dig up something."

I gave a sigh and held out a bag of canary melons. "Here, I brought some fruit."

"We don't need this."

"I'm very tired, do you mind if I sit down for a bit?"

Though she didn't respond, she moved a little to the side. I placed the bag on the kitchen table and pulled out a chair. From my very first visit, I'd always sat in the same seat. On the far side I saw the small window above the kitchen sink. His sister washed dishes noisily. Her head barely came up to the bottom of the window frame.

It seemed that I'd dozed off for a moment. Everything had grown silent, and I felt cold on the outside and warm inside. When I started awake, his sister was standing before me and Han Manu was gazing in our direction from the living room sofa, his crutches propped up against its left arm.

"Did you have something to eat?" she asked me.

My head jerked involuntarily. "What do you mean?"

I skipped lunch every day so that I wouldn't gain weight, but I'd been unable to resist that day and ended up buying a fish cake skewer from a street stall. I'd even had two cups of broth with it. On the days I ate something, I suffered from an overwhelming sense of guilt.

"Why so surprised? You're making me feel bad."

"I didn't really eat. Just barely actually."

"Well, we were about to fry up some eggs."

"For omelets?"

"No, just fried eggs." Then she called toward the living room, "You want two, right?"

"Uh-huh," came the answer.

"We always have an over-easy with salt and an over-hard with ketchup. We eat our eggs like that every day."

I gulped. "You think I could have some, too?"

"Really? How many?"

"I'll have two as well."

She grinned and turned around. She placed a frying pan on the stove and switched on the burner.

"You want them cooked the same way as ours?" she asked as she twisted around to open the refrigerator.

"Yes, the same."

"Okay then! All three the same, coming right up!"

She pulled open the fridge door and reached in three times, grabbing two eggs at a time with her small hand. She set the pale brown eggs on the table, where they started rolling gently. She also took out the ketchup, not a bottle, but small packets you'd get from fast-food restaurants. There were three packets, one for each of us.

After, she brought over some tea on a portable table. She sat across from Han Manu and gave me a look to come join them. As soon as I took a seat, she set down her teacup and saucer with a clatter.

"I never got to see her, but I heard she was no joke," she said.

"Yeah, uh, I guess," Han Manu said.

"But what did you think, oppa?"

"Well, I...," he said, grinning.

They were probably continuing the conversation they'd been having before I arrived. I peered down at the tea set and thought about the eggs I'd just enjoyed. When Han Manu's sister had cracked the first egg with a spoon, I'd flinched. I'd thought about blocking my ears or escaping to the bathroom, but I'd stayed put. She broke the second one, and then the third. I was proud of myself for sitting through six eggs. I hadn't had fried eggs in a long time. I also hadn't seen such old, outdated china in a long time. As if to show that they were part of the same set, the red flowers that were embossed on the teacups decorated the edge of the saucers. Strands of gold and silver gilt ran along the rim of the cup and the inside of the saucer, and the delicate handle of the teacup, which you had to hold lightly with your thumb and index finger, was shaped like a little animal with pricked ears. Everything in their home was like that—old and shabby. In fact, it was full of objects I hadn't seen for a long time.

"But her younger sister is really pretty, too, don't you think?"

The moment she said this, I nearly dropped my teacup. They had been talking about my sister earlier and now she was talking about me. I lowered my face and rubbed the teacup handle with my index finger. That's right, my sister had been no joke. But Han Manu's sister had said I was very pretty, too.

She brought over the melons and started peeling them with a knife, and Han Manu turned on the television. His face, which was turned toward the television, seemed confident, almost exultant. Maybe because his sister was there, or maybe because he knew of my sister's beauty, which his sister knew nothing about. It didn't matter either way. She placed the plate of sliced melon between him and me.

"Have some! You too, Eonni!"

AFTER TAKING his medicine, Han Manu fell asleep on the sofa. His sister turned off the television and glanced at me. It seemed she wanted us to talk in her room.

Her room was very small. She moved the portable table with the plate of melon in from the living room, but there were now two glasses instead of the tea set. She then brought two bottles of beer and a bottle opener, and closed the door. It felt as though we were hiding in a small box.

"I thought a cold beer would be nice."

The beer was refreshing. We drank and munched on the melon.

"Eonni!" she cried, gazing at me with her big, defined eyes. "I don't have a sister, so it feels strange to call you Eonni, but it's nice, too."

Her name was Seonu and she was three years younger than me. She'd been working in sales at a large supermarket ever since she graduated from high school, but she'd had to move to a different supermarket five times in the last four years.

"It's weird, but something happens in this line of work all the time. It's the worst, because we have to undergo new training each time and we don't get paid during the training period. Plus, they always change our days off... I'm sorry, Eonni, but I've got to say this."

I sensed she was going to bring it up.

"It's true I was asleep that night, but I'm positive my brother came home around eleven-thirty. With a bag of sugar twists."

"Sugar twists?"

I gulped once more. For some strange reason, ever since I stepped into their home, I kept salivating and felt hungry.

"When we still lived in that neighborhood, a little place in the corner of the market sold sugar twist doughnuts. My brother would always buy some to bring home. He knew I liked them, so he'd leave them on the table for me. I'd sometimes get up in the middle of the night to eat one or I'd eat them in the morning. I'm just wild about them and that place had the best sugar twists, hands down. But the shop closed at eleven-thirty, so if my brother wanted to buy some, he'd have to leave the chicken shop at eleven. Even his boss knew, so he'd remind my brother and say, 'Aren't you getting sugar twists tonight?' Anyway, there were sugar twists on the table the next morning."

I pictured Han Manu clutching a bag of doughnuts for his sister in one hand and a brick or a rock in the other hand. Was he capable of such a thing?

"But the detective wouldn't believe me. He said anyone could rig something like that. He said anyone who could kill in cold blood would have no problem thinking of those details. So my brother could have planned it all and bought the sugar twists in advance. I was too naive, apparently. He told me I'd been tricked."

Could a murderer really do that? Hold a bag of fresh, still-warm doughnuts while bashing someone's head in? Was it possible?

"What I don't get is, how could buying sugar twists be part of a plan? Are they saying he's been a killer from the time he was in the eighth grade? When he started part-timing at the chicken shop? What a bunch of baloney."

Seonu brought more beer. When I asked her about his leg, a shadow passed over her face.

"He was diagnosed with knee cancer, so he had to get surgery."

Knee cancer?

"I bet this is the first you're hearing about it. That's why they had to amputate above his left knee, but we were lucky the cancer hadn't spread. You can get cancer in your bones, too—it's just that people don't know. I did a ton of research because of my brother. They call bone cancer *sarcoma* or *osteosarcoma*. It affects mostly young people in their teens and twenties, but even when it hurts, they don't realize it's cancer, because they confuse it with growing pains. For my brother, too, it started hurting all of a sudden when he got called away for military service. He told them it hurt really bad, but they thought he was making a fuss for nothing, so he just stayed quiet and put up with the pain. They only took him to the army hospital when he passed out. Then after running some tests, they told him to go home, saying he should go to a bigger hospital. That's how they let him out. How could they be so cruel? If they were going to send him home, shouldn't they have let him go earlier or after they'd finished treating him at least? They were just trying to keep it quiet so they could save their own hides. Even the doctor said if my brother had been treated earlier, he wouldn't have had to amputate. But there's no use in trying to fight something like this. You know what they say, you can't ever win against the military. Or hospitals. But in this case, it involves both of them. All we got in the end was the money for the surgery. Oh, you already finished your drink, Eonni? You must have a high tolerance."

She brought more beer.

"There are different types of sarcoma, but my brother was diagnosed with Ewing sarcoma. James Ewing is the name of the doctor who discovered the cancer. It was named after him. That's why it's called Ewing sarcoma."

"Ewing sarcoma?"

"That's right."

I repeated the name of the cancer, as if it were a tune. Ewing sarcoma...Ewing sarcoma...It sounded almost pretty, even cute, like a tiny mushroom stuck to the bone.

He came down with Ewing sarcoma, ewing ewing
Off went his left knee, ewing ewing
Never again will he drag his feet, ewing ewing

When I asked Seonu about his habit of dragging his feet, she laughed. "How'd you know? It's because his shoes were always too small for him."

But do people drag their feet when their shoes are too small?

"Because as a kid, he couldn't get new shoes, even when his shoes got too small. So he'd wear them with the backs folded in and his heels hanging over the end. That's why he started dragging his feet."

So that's why... But dragging his feet had now become a thing of the past. He'd never be able to shuffle his feet again. It had been decided for him.

"You know, my brother isn't very good at explaining things. Why else would they keep hounding him for that long..."

My brother isn't very good at explaining things... Why else would they keep hounding him... Now that I was getting drunk, I felt sad.

"You see, he and I have different dads..."

Seonu's voice seemed far away, as if it were coming from the opposite side of the world.

"My brother is Han Manu, and I'm Jeong Seonu. We have different dads, but our dads are similar in one way: we don't know where they are. Both of them disappeared. My mom says they were good men, and they felt so bad that they couldn't support the family. That's why they went away. She never says they ran off. She always says they disappeared. My mom's the type of person who thinks like that..."

Her voice was like trickling water or the song of a bird. Things barely heard, like a gentle breeze that grazes your ear, a sound so lovely it could cut your heart, a sound that faded the more you strained to hear it.

"The thing is, I'm so worried about my brother. Him losing his leg—that was nothing. I'm scared he's going to disappear. I'm so scared he's going to disappear one day because he feels bad he can't bring any money home. I used to think that. I used to wonder if my brother broke his back working, because he didn't want to turn out like our dads, so that he wouldn't have to go away. I used to think stupid things like that. What's going to happen to my brother..."

———

"MOM'S COMING," Seonu said, checking her text messages.

As soon as she spoke, Han Manu bolted awake and his expression changed. His glance darted toward me. "Go! Hurry!"

Dull with drink, I didn't know what he meant. Seonu stood in front of me, blocking the way.

"Why are you telling her to go?"

"Didn't you say Mom was coming? Don't you know how upset she'll get if she sees these people coming around again? Did you hear me? Get out! Hurry!"

"Then we can just say she isn't one of them! We can say it's someone I know!" Seonu said, choking back sobs. "Eonni hasn't done anything wrong, so why are you telling her to go?"

All at once, I felt sad. I wanted to throw a fit. I didn't want to hold back any longer. Even before I'd made up my mind to cry, tears rolled down my cheeks. Grimacing, Han Manu looked from his sister, who was close to crying, to me, who was now crying in earnest.

"What's the matter with you two? . . . Fine, whatever."

Seonu turned and hugged me. "Eonni, you don't have to go. Don't cry. My brother's being mean."

Like a child, I rubbed my eyes with my fists, fully aware that I was smearing my makeup. Look up laws about employment for those with disabilities. Find businesses that provide special employment opportunities. Despite being drunk, these were the thoughts I had. I couldn't let him watch television all day and then disappear. I needed to find a way for him to earn some money.

Some lives are unfair for no apparent reason, but we carry on, completely unaware, like miserable vermin. As I had half suspected, their mother, who worked in a restaurant kitchen, had dwarfism. She was very small, as if Seonu had been shrunken down much more severely. For some strange reason, when I saw their mother, it became very clear where I was supposed to go and what I was supposed to do. Even my direction in life became certain. First of all, I could no longer live with my mother. In no way could she ever become involved. But I'd go back to her one day. One day I would be back.

GOD, 2015

●

HELLO, DOCTOR. It's so nice to finally meet you. It's such an honor.

I really wanted to see you. You don't know how long I waited to get an appointment. I read your column in the paper every week, by the way. And I was so moved by your book *Grief, a Beautiful Goodbye*. I've been a fan ever since. Is it silly of me to call myself a fan? I hope you don't mind. Oh, thank you for being so gracious.

———

SHALL I start then? Three years ago, I went through a very difficult time... Did you hear about it by any chance, Doctor? Ah, you did. It was all over the news, after all. Pardon me? You heard from someone you know? Yes, I guess most people would know. After that horrible...that horrible...I had a very difficult time... It was terrible. How could it not be? After going through that, I—sorry, I'm so sorry. No, no, I'm fine. It'll pass soon. I'm doing better now. A lot better. If you'll hold on for a bit. Just a little bit...

Okay, why don't I start over? I'm fine now. Yes, much better. These days I clear my mind by reading and writing poetry every morning. You mean you didn't know I write poetry? I made my official debut as a poet, actually. Your church ran my work twice in their weekly bulletin. Pardon? How do I know which church you attend? How could anyone not know—a famous doctor like yourself! Oh, you haven't been going much these days? Of course, that'll happen when you're busy. It's understandable for someone as busy as you are. Still, I do hope you'll try your best to attend this Sunday.

So anyway, after that...that incident...ah, I wonder what's wrong with me? After that incident, through the grace of God, I started writing poems. How it all started was...I became very depressed after I had the baby. Postpartum depression...Many new moms get it, apparently, especially the sensitive ones. Oh, the...baby? Do I have to talk about her? My baby...Yebin...Shin Yebin...She was an angel, a truly beautiful baby. Everyone who saw her said they'd never seen a more beautiful baby. My father-in-law, who doesn't know how to compliment anyone, even he said, "My son and daughter-in-law are lookers, but they don't hold a candle to Yebin!" Oh, she was unbelievably beautiful. That girl...that girl was beautiful, too...She must have been...as a baby...just as beautiful...

That girl? Oh, I got confused for a second. That girl...I mean, Yebin...Yes, Yebin. My husband was completely smitten with her. With Yebin, our daughter. When I first told him I was pregnant, he didn't seem that—he was happy, of course, but only as much as a man might get, not any more than that, so who knew he'd go completely mad for her? From the moment she was born, he did a total one-eighty. It was to the point...Ah, it makes me think of that day, the day he was putting her to sleep. Okay, I'll try to explain. Yebin was an extremely fussy baby. If she hadn't been so beautiful, I probably would have lost it and given her a spanking. She was a terrible sleeper, too. She wouldn't fall asleep unless you held her, and even then, you had to rock her for a long time before she'd finally fall asleep. But that day, he held her for a long time, rocking her to sleep. I had no idea he could be so patient... You see, he has a bit of a temper and he's not the type to bend over backward for anyone. That day, though... I couldn't believe how long he held her, trying to put her to sleep, and as he was about to lay her down in the crib...he...he stopped and gazed at her for a long time...a very long time. He didn't know I was watching. If he'd known, he would have never done that. Then he put his lips on her forehead and stayed that way again for a long time. And then...and then...he started crying. Quietly, without making a sound. Why did he cry? I'd never seen him cry before. I'd known him since high school— though I didn't see him when he went to America for school, obviously—but he wasn't one to cry. I'm sure he did sometimes, but I never saw it, since he never did it in front of me or anybody else. But then that day, because he thought no one was there, because he didn't know I was watching... But what was there to cry about? What on earth was there to be sad about? When I saw that, I...got the chills. It was horrible. What do you mean why, Doctor? You mean you don't find it horrible? I found it so awful that I just wanted...to die. That's the only thought I had. Why? I don't know. All I know is that I wanted to die. Because I was depressed. I was so depressed I wanted to die. I wanted to bash my head...against the bathroom tiles...until it cracked open like that time...cranial injury...to just die. The same way...I felt I could do it.

Yes, it was serious, very serious, Doctor. Because I was so depressed, many people from church came by to help me and to pray for me. One was an older woman, a poet, who told me how to heal your mind through poetry. She even gave me a book of poems she'd written. To be honest, though, I couldn't stand her at first. Her fake front teeth looked so sharp, almost sawlike, and gave off a bluish glint each time she smiled...They got on my nerves so much I had nightmares about getting sucked up into a saw blade. You won't believe how many times I told her she didn't have to come around anymore, but she's the type who can't take no for an answer. Once she even brought a horde of poets along and put on a reading. The whole thing made me shudder! I was so depressed I could die, but she kept harassing and tormenting me with nonsense, insisting that I draw out the poetry from within, that she'd publish my poems in her magazine...What did she take me for?

Was she trying to use me to save her doomed magazine? I couldn't help being suspicious...And her poetry wasn't even good. For someone who's been writing poetry for as long as she has, it was so...I tried to avoid her for a long time...

Anyway, that was that...yes, the horrible incident happened during this time. That idiotic babysitter, how could she have pushed the stroller all the way home without realizing the baby wasn't even inside? If I owned a gun that didn't make a sound, I would have just...right then and there...And you think the police were any better? Instead of carrying out a proper investigation, they'd come by to talk about grudges and financial problems, as if trying to dig up some big secret we were hiding. All they did was ask questions that had nothing to do with the situation, those dumb useless cops...But what I found absolutely unbelievable was my in-laws' response. Instead of demanding that the police do their job, my in-laws ordered them to stop the investigation. I have no idea why they did that. Maybe my father-in-law had something to hide? Or could it have had something to do with that incident from long ago...Sorry, I don't want to talk about that. Oh, I'm getting angry again. Do you know what my mother-in-law said to me then? She said she wouldn't let the family name be dragged through the mud and asked if we couldn't just have another baby...What kind of crazy...Are those the words of a sane person? If I think about what she said, my blood boils and I can't see straight. It feels as if I've got my face in a fire. Is my face red right now? Doctor? Is everything all right? Do you mind if I go to the bathroom? I'll be right back. Excuse me.

THANK YOU for waiting, Doctor. But I just thought of something while I was in the bathroom—do you mind if I ask you about it? You know the term *cold-blooded*, Doctor? Yes, *cold-blooded*. You know, people with little or no emotion. Have you met anyone like that before? You must have, since you've treated so many patients. It's a matter of degree, you say? I'm talking about people who are extremely cold-blooded. Are they born like that or is it something that's learned as they grow up? It can be both? It can be caused by a combination of factors?

Oh, the reason I bring this up is, sometimes in life, you come across people like that. Pardon me? Anyone in my circle? No, no, I don't mean anyone close to me, but you know how you exchange small talk with people sometimes, but certain ones will give you the chills? The poet? Oh, gosh, no, she's the complete opposite! Her problem is that she's too emotional. Plus, she's a woman. Of course, I don't mean to imply that women can't be cold-blooded. Have I ever met a man who was cold-blooded? No, it's not that... Maybe we should discuss something else. I'm getting a little upset. To be honest, I don't think all this talk is going to help... Just talk about it comfortably? About what? Talk about what comfortably? How am I supposed to do that? All right, I'll try not to get so worked up... stay calm... let it go... just let it go... nice and slow...

Fine then, I won't hold back, Doctor. So someone who's cold-blooded... What I want to say about that is, people like that make you feel like they're not really listening to you. They're listening, but it's like talking to a brick wall, as if your words are just bouncing off. Do you know that feeling, Doctor? Also... I can't remember, now that I'm trying to talk about it... Ah, yes, they can never admit they're wrong! Yes, I've noticed that about them. They do something wrong, and then they deny everything and say it wasn't their fault. Anyone would say it's a hundred percent their fault, but they keep insisting they did nothing wrong, but what's more unbelievable is that they say it's *your* fault and try to pin everything on you. That will really drive you crazy. I tell you, these people can be so irrational I sometimes wonder if they're actually nuts. But what's more horrible is that they think girls are their playthings, dolls they can use and control, and if you don't do what they want, they look at you in the most horrible, atrocious way. It's torture. They're perfectly fine, since they have no emotions, and I'm the one who's going crazy over here, those bastards. And when they fool around, it's with young girls, nineteen-, twenty-year-olds, always around the same age as that girl...

DOCTOR, WHY are you looking at me like that? Oh, who am I talking about? What do you mean who? No, I'm not talking about anyone specific. I just mentioned what comes to mind when I think of someone being cold-blooded. Yes, about people like that in general...Yes, of course I was speaking generally. No, I wasn't talking from personal experience, definitely not. I just spoke aloud what came to mind, that's all. And I used a bit of my imagination, too. Since I write poetry, I tend to have a more active imagination than other people. I have a knack for seeing into people's motives and I'm quite empathetic, too.

Pardon me? Whose husband? My husband? Why are you mentioning him all of a sudden? Ah, yes, I'm very worried about him. He was utterly devoted to Yebin. Until she came along, I had no idea he could be that way. I didn't think he even wanted a baby, but from the day she was born, he went through a complete transformation...Ah, did I mention that already? Yes, my baby...she wasn't a year old when it happened...she'd be three now...or would she be four? The clothes and shoes I'd bought for her...she never got to try them on, not once...Even her baby room is exactly the same as it was then. It's because he won't let me clear anything away. For a while, he shut himself in her room and didn't come out. I'm worried sick about him. I am. And I don't think he's really working these days. You see, he's always been so meticulous about his work. He could have gone all the way to the top—everyone believed he could—but he's let it all go and been carrying on like this for the past several years. I don't know how long he plans to ruin his life. I'm beyond worried now. It's pathetic. If he decides to ruin his life completely, if he loses his job...of course I'm worried. How could I not be? Do I understand him? Obviously! But why do you ask me that, Doctor? If I can't understand him, then who can? I understand him perfectly. He doesn't want to have another baby. On that matter, I couldn't agree with him more. I have absolutely no desire to give my in-laws another grandchild. *You can always have another baby, can't you?* Unbelievable.

Through poetry, at least I'm moving toward healing, but he has no desire to get better. Plus, he doesn't even go to church these days. Doctor, why don't you try going to church this Sunday? Can you promise me? No? People like that...people like my husband, souls who aren't saved...I feel sorry for them. As I read and recite and write poetry, I feel a peace and exuberance, as if I'm meeting with the Lord. Through that person—that woman poet with the fake front teeth—I realized the Lord moved heaven and earth to save me. Yebin...Back then when that happened, I couldn't see. I couldn't understand His ways, how He was working, even through that situation. But now I know He uses everything that has ever happened to me to bring about His saving work. I see it now. I'm completely weak and powerless before Him. Doctor, have you ever tasted this deep and perfect joy of having received what the Lord has willed—whether it's happiness or suffering—and of gladly receiving whatever He pleases, even to

the point of death? Doctor, do you know the plea-
sure of translating that joy into poetry? Poetry to
me is His Word, and His Word is poetry. It's been
tough, because everyone I meet these days asks me
if I can write something for their Sunday bulletin or
weekly insert and I have a hard time saying no. But
if my poems can help praise God's great love even
a little…I try to write with that kind of attitude in
mind, to respond to the Lord in that way. Doctor, do
you think you could wait a bit while I pray?

Lord Jesus, our loving Jesus, we give you thanks
for this day…

I ALWAYS feel better after praying, as if a load's been
taken off my chest. My head hurts less, too. Yes,
I get nasty headaches. At night, they get so bad I
can't sleep unless I take some sleeping pills, but even
then, I feel like I can finally fall asleep only after I
pray. No, I don't take sleeping pills every night. I'm
fine, Doctor. My husband's the problem. It would
be nice if he could see you, but he'll never agree to
something like this. He's going to get much worse.
I already know. Once at night, when I was praying
by myself, the Lord told me very clearly, as if He'd
written to me. He said my husband's soul will be led

to the valley of the shadow of death. Now I'll recite for you the poem I wrote down after He dictated it to me.

> *A cracked rabbit skull*
> *A lion now a pocket of pus*
> *How amazing is His grace, eunhae eunhae eunhae**
> *The sun is shrouded with ashes*
> *The black heaven covers the frozen earth*
> *O Sing to Him, eunhae eunhae eunhae*

Doctor, do you know what this poem means? Do you know what it means to sing "eunhaeeunhaeeunhae" even when the head cracks open and the body rots away, when the sun disappears and the ground freezes over? It means there's no need for us to do anything else except praise Him and worship Him and pray to Him and hunger for salvation. It means we should do nothing else. We have nothing, absolutely nothing of our own, and everything we have is borrowed from Him. Though I am already saved— oh, Lord Jesus, thank you, Lord of Grace—salvation isn't something we can receive in one try. We must receive His salvation every minute, every hour. I

---

* The translation of *eunhae* is *grace*.

desperately pray that you, Doctor, will receive His salvation...A life that isn't saved is a cursed life. A cursed life can't ever die or be severed, it will go on for eternity in the fires of hell. You must grasp that truth with all your heart and all your mind, Doctor. I'll pray for you every day. Let us pray.

SARCOMA, 2017

THE POST-SYMPOSIUM dinner was held at a nearby barbeque restaurant. All the participants filed in one after another to sit at tables that had been put together in a long line. I ended up somewhere in the middle with my back against the wall. As soon as the server brought over the side dishes and place settings, everyone became busy collecting their cutlery and plates. I wiped my hands with a hot towel and watched a graduate student place pork belly strips on the hot grill.

The evening news was playing on the television hanging on the opposite wall. As I mixed the dipping sauce for the meat, a word that the news anchor said pierced through the clamor and fixed itself into my mind. I raised my head.

On the screen was a skater racing around an oval ice rink. In a sober voice, the anchor announced that an athlete on the national short track team had passed away from osteosarcoma of the shoulder. "This cancer, which was discovered while he was being treated for an elbow injury, is called sarcoma or osteosarcoma..."

Sarcoma. Though the word was unfamiliar, it was something I'd heard maybe once before. How did I even know it? I sank into thought. When everything grew quiet, I glanced around to find all eyes on me. My thesis adviser, who was seated diagonally across from me, seemed to have asked me something. When I looked to the lecturer sitting next to me, he prompted, "What will you have? To drink?" I picked up my shot glass and held it out toward my adviser. Once it was filled, we clinked glasses together. I realized then that my midterm thesis defense was coming up, and in that instant, a memory slithered up my belly like a snake: the National Library and Da-on.

It must have been in the middle of November of last year. I ran into Da-on in front of the lockers on the ground floor of the library.

"Sanghui eonni!" she called.

If she hadn't called out to me, I probably wouldn't have recognized her. It had been ten years since I'd seen her last on the steps of the university library. Ten years was a long time, but still Da-on's transformation was so drastic I couldn't help being shocked. She now had glasses and short curly hair, and she'd put on a lot of weight. She was wearing a parka the color of eggplant with black trousers, but the large parka was lumpy, as if it had been stuffed with real eggplants. And because she was in sneakers, she seemed to have gotten shorter. At a glance, she appeared three or four years older than me, but close up, her no-makeup skin was bright and rosy. I might have been able to recognize her more easily, if I hadn't run into her outside the university library. After all, it wouldn't have been a stretch to accept that high school Da-on, who had looked like a country girl, had become someone resembling a country woman, if the bizarre image of the girl in the yellow dress hadn't been wedged in between.

But why had Da-on brought up sarcoma that day? I tried to recall the context, but everything was a haze. I couldn't remember talking about the disease at all. But in my mind, I could still see the serious expression on Da-on's face as she uttered the word *sarcoma*. Had she told me about someone's diagnosis?

As people drank, the restaurant grew increasingly noisy. I couldn't hear the television at all, despite the fact that the volume was turned up high. Someone complained it was too loud, and used an app on their phone to turn off the television, but it was still noisy and I could no longer think of anything else. It was only on the subway on my way home that I managed to recall most of the details from the last time I'd run into Da-on.

THAT DAY I had to go to the National Library to photocopy some research material I needed for my thesis. I put my bag in a locker and was about to step through the entrance gate when I realized I hadn't brought my wallet. I went back to the locker and rummaged through my bag, but my wallet wasn't there. I'd forgotten it at home. Flustered, I was searching through the pockets of my coat when someone called, "Sanghui eonni!"

"What are you looking for?" Da-on asked, picking up as if we'd seen each other only the day before.

I told her I'd left my wallet at home.

"As long as you didn't lose it," she said. She pulled out her wallet, thinking I needed some money.

"It's not that," I said. "My library card's in my wallet."

"Then you can just ask for a day pass. It'll be ready right away."

Again, I told her it wasn't that. I needed an ID card to get a day pass, and my ID card was also in my wallet.

"Oh, I see," Da-on said with a loud ringing laugh.

I couldn't help being surprised once more.

"Why do you have to go to the library? Can I help with anything?"

"Actually, I need to photocopy some things."

"I can do it for you."

"Well, it's a bit complicated to find the material."

"Then do you want to just take my library card and copy everything yourself?"

What she suggested was indeed the best possible option. If you scanned your card when entering the library, you didn't need to go through the process of verifying your identity. This, obviously, was the most convenient arrangement for me, but I felt bad. However, Da-on assured me it was no problem and handed me her library card.

"Then I'll be back as soon as I'm done copying everything. Do you want to go wait somewhere comfortable?"

"I'll be in the lounge on this floor. Take your time."

And so I took Da-on's library card and went inside.

WHEN I returned with the copies, Da-on was standing by the lounge window, talking on the phone. I overheard a name that sounded familiar. It would have been better not to have heard it at all. In a voice brimming with happiness, I'd heard her ask, "How's Hye-eun, Mother?" It had sounded as if she'd said, "How's Hae-on?"

Hye-eun and Hae-on. The names sounded nearly identical. "Oh, really?" Da-on said, with a loud laugh. I backed away. Though I'd had no intention of eavesdropping, I somehow felt I needed to hide the fact that I'd heard. A vague but certain fear crept over me. When she finished her conversation and glanced back, I was able to approach her from a safe distance.

"You're done?" she asked with a smile.

"Thanks to you," I said, as I handed back her library card.

"After sitting here for a while, I started feeling a little weird."

At her words, I glanced at the sofas placed around the lounge. Most of the people there were elderly men with a sober, dignified bearing. Gravelly voices that sounded a little short of breath, a musty odor with a subtle whiff of aftershave, and the intense smell of instant coffee mix filled the air. Da-on launched into several amusing anecdotes. For example, about the tactic of one old man, always respectably dressed, who pretends to stumble and then cuts in front of young people in the cafeteria line, so that he can nab the food tray with the biggest serving of his favorite side dish. Or the arguments that break out sometimes among the elderly men and the absurd claims they'd each make. Or the pointless disputes that would drag on and on until some random patriotic conclusion would decide everything at once. All the stories were of this sort. For some reason, they didn't sit well with me.

"It sounds like you come here often," I said, trying to change the subject.

"You could say that."

I realized I'd only met Da-on at either the literary club or the library, at spaces that had to do with language.

"Are you studying for something?" I asked her.

"No ... I'm trying to write something."

"Write what? Poetry?"

Da-on shook her head. "No, Eonni. Not poetry. I can't write poems."

She hesitated, registering the questioning look in my eyes. Then a moment later she said, "I guess I'm writing something like a confession?"

Before I could say anything more, she took up the subject of the elderly men again. Their stubbornness; their irritability; their obsession over minor details; their blurting of certain words, as if supplied by a built-in mechanism; their tendency to move in perfect order, like birds flying in formation.

"I swear, this place is more like a museum than a library," Da-on said, biting her lip.

The word *museum* made me think of taxidermy specimens, which then made me recall the shrouded body of my father. Without thinking, I mumbled, "If my father were still alive, he would have become one of these men for sure."

"Your father passed away?" Da-on asked, surprised.

"From liver cancer. In the spring two years ago," I said briefly.

Shortly after, I talked about the combativeness that had defined his life, how suffocated I'd felt by his narrow-mindedness. Because of him, I had gone to teachers' college and become a teacher, and after he passed away, I'd quit my teaching job and entered graduate school. I'd never hated my father for these reasons, but I'd also never loved him either.

"And that still confuses me," I said.

After I said those words, I grew even more confused. It seemed there was nothing different about the way I'd viewed my father until now from the way Da-on viewed these elderly people in the lounge. Still, I felt uncomfortable listening to her pick apart their every action. Had my father been like these men? Was that all he'd been?

"It's natural to feel confused by things you can't change," Da-on said like a wise sage.

"You think?" I murmured vaguely.

"Death carves a clear line between the dead and the living," she said in a solemn tone. "The dead are over there and the rest of us are over here. When someone dies, no matter how great they were, it's like drawing a permanent line between that person and the rest of humanity. If birth means begging to join the side of the living, then death has the power to kick everyone out. That's why I think death, with its power to sever things forever, is far more objective, more dignified, than birth, which is the starting point of everything." Da-on spoke calmly, as if she were reading from a book.

Da-on had walked this path for a long time. She had mulled over these thoughts until no rough edges remained, to the extent that her views on death seemed more terrifying, more resigned, than ones held by those on death's doorstep.

"Death turns us into junk. In the blink of an eye, we become meaningless, like scraps."

As soon as I heard this, I thought of Hae-on. When I recalled her beauty, which had turned us into scraps in an instant, a beauty so staggering I found myself wondering if it had actually existed, my heart surged.

"Some people have that effect on others, even when they're alive. For example..." I hesitated for a moment and said her name. "Hae-on, your sister. When we were with her, we were just scraps. We were nothing."

Da-on smiled. It was closer to a grimace, like the one I'd seen on her face at the library café a long time ago.

"Sanghui eonni, did I ever tell you? We changed my sister's name."

When I told her she hadn't, she explained that Hae-on had originally been named Hye-eun. "But our dad—"

I tried my best to pay attention to what she was saying, but I couldn't. What I'd overheard Da-on say on the phone kept ringing in my ears. *How's Hye-eun, Mother...* Had she said Hye-eun or Hae-on? Hye-eun... Hae-on... Mother... I realized Da-on was staring at me. In order to appear as though I were listening, I nodded.

"My mother still thinks that... believe it or not...," she said, and closed her mouth.

I didn't know what her mother still thought, but one thing was clear: in the lives of both Da-on and her mother, there was now a different Hye-eun or Hae-on. And I couldn't help but find this fact chilling.

THE TALK about sarcoma didn't come up in the lounge. We each got our bags from the lockers and headed out of the building. Da-on said she wanted to have a cigarette, so we walked toward the benches in the smoking area. When I asked her if she was free, saying that I wanted to treat her to dinner, she agreed readily.

"Do you drink?" I asked.

"Of course," she said, with a laugh.

"Then I'll buy you a drink, too."

She laughed again. She seemed to be saying, You go ahead and do that and I'll keep laughing. It was nice to see her in a lighthearted mood, but I felt depressed all the same.

While Da-on had a cigarette, I couldn't stop thinking of the other Hye-eun or Hae-on she had mentioned on the phone. I don't know why Yun Taerim suddenly came to mind just then. Maybe it was because Da-on had asked me ten years ago if I kept in touch with Taerim. I'd told her then that I sometimes saw her at alumni meet-ups. Da-on had asked for my number then, but she hadn't called once after that, not even to request Yun Taerim's contact information.

Da-on finished her cigarette and lit another one. When smoking became banned in many public spaces, more and more people began to smoke several cigarettes at once, one after another. When had Da-on started smoking? Did she want Taerim's phone number, perhaps? I hadn't seen Taerim for a long time. Before she got married to Shin Jeongjun, she had shown up to pass out wedding invitations, but she never returned after that. We believed it was because she resented us, since none of us had attended her wedding.

Da-on looked like she was enjoying her cigarette. A few years after Taerim's wedding, I'd heard at another alumni meet-up that her baby girl had been abducted. It was no rumor; it was the truth. The babysitter had taken the baby for a short walk in the stroller, but when she returned to the apartment, the baby was gone. How had she failed to notice that the baby was missing while she pushed the stroller home? She said she'd had no idea. The canopy had been pulled down, and the stroller hadn't felt any lighter. The bottom storage basket had been loaded with baby things and she'd hung a shopping bag filled with milk, fruit, and juice she'd bought at the organics store on the handle. After retracing the babysitter's steps, the police identified the organics store as the most likely location where the kidnapping had taken place. The babysitter had parked the stroller at the end of the counter in the corner and bickered a little with an employee.

"So basically," said an alumna, drawing a line on the table with her finger. "Say this is the counter and this side here is the rest of the store." She then jabbed a corner near one end of the line and said, "She parked the stroller around here."

Because the security camera was pointed toward the counter on the customer side, the area right behind the camera was a blind spot. The alumna said it must have been at that moment that someone took the baby from the stroller. Right then, I became overcome with a strong sense of déjà vu, and I couldn't block out the memory of kids drawing sketches and scrawling numbers on the chalkboard after Hae-on had died, each trying to figure out whether Shin Jeongjun or Han Manu was the culprit. Did I think of Taerim now because of that sense of déjà vu, because Da-on had asked last time if I still talked to her?

Da-on stubbed out her cigarette in the ashtray and asked, "Eonni, do you believe in God?"

"God?" I repeated. "I don't think so. How about you?"

"Not yet."

"Does that mean you might believe later?"

"No," she said. "I want to believe...but I can't. How can I, when things I can't possibly understand are happening all over the world?"

Just as she had in the library lounge when she talked about the elderly people, she started firing off examples I could barely get the gist of.

"For example, somewhere in the world, a girl is born. She's born into a family so poor she often goes hungry. She's beaten, rummages through garbage for food, gets sick, and goes blind. When she's eleven years old, she is gang-raped, stabbed repeatedly, and murdered. Then her body is thrown out in the same garbage dump where she'd rummaged for food her whole life. How can you believe in a god after that?"

At first, I didn't understand why Da-on was telling me this, but I became fascinated the more I listened. It wasn't what she talked about that I found fascinating; it was her tone, her attitude. I sensed a terrible loneliness, not just because Da-on appeared lonely, but because she seemed to be in a state of extreme isolation. Either by choice or by force, she had become completely cut off from everyone.

Da-on took a deep breath, as if trying to calm herself, and went on. "Here's another example. Somewhere in the world, a boy is born as the eldest son in a poor family. He has a mother with dwarfism and a younger sister, and since there's no money for new shoes, he drags his feet, because he has to fold down the backs of his small shoes. From the time he's eleven, he needs to work while attending school to make some extra money. Then at the age of eighteen, he's falsely accused of murder, beaten by the police, blamed by everyone, and kicked out of school. When he starts his military service, he is diagnosed with sarcoma—" (this is when I heard that word for the first time) "—has his leg amputated and gets out of the military on a disability discharge. He starts working at a laundry plant, is badly burned as a presser, and discovers that his sarcoma has spread to his lungs and then dies at the age of twenty-nine. How can anyone call this divine providence?"

I could sense that Da-on had desperately wanted to confide in someone for a long time, but something was holding her back, and she could only brood on the periphery of that subject.

"Unless we can confidently say that everything is divine providence—even when the watchtower burns down and the ship sinks—we can't say we believe in God. I can't ever say all this is divine providence, not in a million years! It's not providence—it's ignorance! We should be saying everything is divine ignorance, that it's God who doesn't know—"

Right then, Da-on's cell phone rang. She checked the incoming number and stood up from the bench. I sensed she wanted some privacy. She moved off far enough so that she wouldn't be overheard and talked on the phone with her back turned to me.

The words Da-on had spewed weren't all non-sense. They hinted at something, gleaming faintly. *Then at the age of eighteen, he's falsely accused of murder...* Could she have meant... Before I could remember his name, the opening words of the song came to mind. "Han maneun i sesang..." This life full of misery. That's right, Han Manu. Had she been talking about him, the boy who'd been in my grade? Was he the one who had died from sarcoma at the age of twenty-nine?

"Sorry, Eonni," Da-on said, after she'd hung up. "I really wish we could've had dinner together at least once, but I have to go. Something's come up."

But judging from Da-on's bright expression, whatever had happened didn't seem like bad news.

"Maybe you don't believe in God," Da-on said with a playful smile. "But how about poetry? You believe in poetry, right?"

"Of course," I said, smiling.

I wanted to tell Da-on a story about my mother I'd just remembered. After my father passed away, my mother would often say, as she skimmed the hardened fat off the top of the short rib soup or soy sauce braised beef, "If the fat didn't rise to the top, your father would have passed away a lot earlier."

"If the fat didn't rise to the top? What's that supposed to mean?" Da-on asked.

"It was her way of saying she missed him. Like what the song says, if the sea was land, there would be no goodbyes or crying at the dock..."

At my words, laughter burst from Da-on's mouth, high and clear, like the bell of a bicycle.

"Mothers really are something, don't you think? That's probably the most honest mourning I've ever heard."

"To skim the fat for someone she never skimped on?"

"*To skim the fat* and *never skimped on*? I told you you're a poet!"

We had a good laugh and got to our feet, as if we'd just remembered something. We waved goodbye to each other, as though we were going to see each other again the next day. I wasn't able to ask her anything— not where she lived, not her phone number. Even if I had asked, she probably wouldn't have told me.

AFTERWARD, I went to the National Library regularly and decided I might as well work on my thesis there. I looked for Da-on each time, but despite what she'd said about going there often, she was nowhere to be seen. Then one day it came to me. After I'd run into Da-on, she'd never come back to the library, and never again would she come back, even in the future. There would be no reason for her to have a cigarette near the benches in the smoking area.

She'd said she wished we could have had dinner together at least once. At the time, my head had been filled with thoughts of Yun Taerim and Han Manu, and so I didn't pay much attention to what she said, but when I think back, she was telling me she had no intention of ever seeing me again. *At least once.* In other words, *never again.* Da-on was avoiding me. Not just me, but anyone who knew about the incident from long ago. As she should. She would want to be cut off from the rest of the world, to be forgotten. Is that why she had gained weight, put on glasses, and concealed herself in a large parka the color of egg-plant, as if she meant to hide herself in a cocoon? In case someone might recognize her?

As I got off the subway, I told myself that all these thoughts might be ridiculous, baseless spec-ulations. But if they weren't, if my hunch turned out to be true, what had happened in the summer of the Korea-Japan World Cup wasn't over. And it never will be. It will go on endlessly, until the end of Da-on's life, or maybe beyond that. Not being able to put an end to an incident so horrific—I couldn't begin to imagine that kind of weight on a life.

DUSK, 2019

●

FOR A long time, I didn't have the nerve to go inside the laundry plant where Han Manu worked. I'd
gone there many times, but I'd been so terrified by
the deafening drone that I'd had to turn around.

That day, when I finally worked up the courage
to step through the open door of the facility, the air
inside was hot and muggy. Laundry bins hit the
ground with a boom and linens cracked as they were
pulled taut. I stepped farther inside, thinking I could
bear the noises. Then I heard a bell clashing, a knife
being sharpened, objects stabbed again and again
by an awl, gasps and shrieks—they entered my ears

and became amplified, swelling before my eyes until I couldn't take another step forward.

As I was about to turn to leave, I caught sight of Han Manu between the garments moving on the overhead conveyor belt. The moment I saw his long, tranquil face, a small miracle occurred. The terrible noises died down. No, it would be more correct to say the nature of the noises changed. What had been like the screeching of metal on metal converged, ballooning like a giant cloud, until it gradually deflated. Each noise assumed its original sound, becoming ordinary once more. I heard the whir of the washers, the rattling of the dryers, the beeping of timers, and the whoosh of the steam iron. No longer were they the roars that had tried to attack and beat me, but sounds restored to their proper shapes, like tools organized neatly in a tool box. I listened, like someone hearing these sounds for the first time. That's right, you're supposed to hear them, not see them, I chanted calmly to myself. Still, it was truly noisy inside the facility.

I stepped into the narrow aisle. I passed by old men sorting the dirty laundry and checking their contamination level, old women in rubber gloves who were scrubbing the soiled spots with detergent, and middle-aged women swiftly putting dress shirts and suit jackets on body forms that went around in a circle. According to Seonu, when Han Manu first started working at the plant, he'd been assigned these simple tasks as well. But now, he was stationed where the dummies made their last stop. The pressing cabinet, shaped like a body form, ironed the front and back of the garment at the same time, then it was removed and placed before Han Manu. Seated in a chair, he spread the garment on the ironing board and delicately pressed the parts that needed to be redone with a hand iron. Just as the chicken shop owner had said, Han Manu was a good worker. He held the iron in his right hand, and with his left hand gently lifted the shirt collar, cuffs, front hem, and interlining as he worked, but his movements were so light and nimble that it was hard to believe what Seonu had said, about his hand and arm being covered with blisters from burn injuries he'd suffered. The iron seemed a natural part of his right arm, or even an extension of it, not something that was hot or dangerous. The clothes that passed through his hands were hung on hangers, covered with plastic, and then carried away on an overhead conveyer belt.

A short while later, he moved to a different station to press the linens. With a crutch wedged under his left arm, he held, like a rifle, a long steam iron connected to a boiler in his right hand. Once he clipped the sheet to the rack and it became completely spread out, he limped sideways, pushing and pulling the iron in a straight line. The precision of his work was immediately apparent on the sheet. As he shuffled to the side while moving his iron back and forth, the wrinkled sheet that had just come out of the dryer became perfectly smooth. To my eyes, he didn't appear to be ironing; it seemed he was weaving a brand-new sheet. I watched him work for a long time. His head, now bald from chemotherapy, shone through the steam spewing from the iron, and dazzling new linen sprang from his graceful movements. When he turned and tripped, falling on the bumpy floor of the facility, and even after he died, I saw that scene in my mind, ever so clearly, for a very long time.

I DIDN'T go to his funeral. It had been a long time since I'd lost touch with Seonu. But there are times I miss the siblings so much I can hardly bear it. I miss the smell of simmering pork bones that had hung in the air of their home, and I even miss their mother, who with her short stubby fingers had marinated the cabbage that would go in the soup. They would still be living in the same place in Suite 301 of Building A, but I can't set foot in their home, or get my shoes repaired at the small shop in the building in front of their home. Neither can I listen to the singing of hymns drifting out from the church on the second floor. I won't be able to see Seonu or her mother for a long time. I might never be able to see them again.

I know better than anyone that they're good people. But if by any chance Shin Jeongjun and Yun Taerim tell the police about the incident from long ago—I doubt they ever will, but if they decide to come clean—the first thing the police will do is track down Han Manu's family. And since he has died, they will question his mother and sister, monitoring their every movement. While answering the police's various questions, they might mention me. In their open, good-natured way, they might describe when I had first come looking for them, how we had set our doubts to rest, how we had grown close since then. Then the police will lock their sights on me.

I still can't help but wonder, do our lives truly hold no meaning? Even if you try desperately to find it, to contrive some kind of meaning, is it true that what's not there isn't there? Does life leave only misery behind? Could the fact that we're alive—the fact that we're in this life where joy and terror and peace and danger mingle—couldn't that itself be the meaning of life? Hadn't Han Manu, with an iron in one hand and a crutch wedged under his other arm, been more alive than anyone in this world, more alive than the cancer cells that had spread to his lungs? Hadn't my sister Hae-on—as she sat with her feet on the sofa or car seat, her knees spread with not a thought in her head, with absolutely no clue as to the inappropriateness of her actions— been warm and exquisitely alive, just like a bird about to take flight? Couldn't each moment we're living now be the meaning of life?

THEY ARE gone now. But through the death of Han Manu, I was able to mourn my sister. I finally understood that her life, just like his, was painfully snuffed out; it wasn't just her perfect beauty that was snuffed out but her very essence. They died, but I'm alive. To be alive—if this indeed is enough, I won't think about anything else from now on. I'm still here and each day I carry on. With me are my mother and little Hye-eun, a guilt no one knows about and an abiding loneliness.

Sometimes I think about the rage that had seethed within me the first time I'd visited Han Manu. I think about the curses I'd heaped on him, how I'd shrieked that his amputated leg meant he was being punished, that his illness wouldn't stop there. I recall the moment he'd said *knees*, sitting with his back turned to the small kitchen window. I recall his grinning face. His grin that had smoothed out his pinched face that resembled a pickle, turning it into a bright canary melon instead, his grin I'd looked upon heartlessly while feeling a violent hatred, his naive, foolish grin that had revealed his feelings for a certain girl.

I picture the scene in my mind. An eighteen-year-old boy waits at the intersection on his delivery scooter. Behind the boy sits a pretty girl with crimson lips and eyes that tilt up at the corners. When the traffic lights change, the scooter comes to life and her hands grasp his sides. Her hands are warm and soft like feathers. *She's wearing a tank top with shorts*, she says, her breath grazing his ear. His creased cheeks become flushed with a happiness he'd never once felt in his brief life. Beneath it all, an unknown terror is lurking. He races across the intersection brimming with joy and terror, almost soaring into the radiant June dusk.

KWON YEO-SUN was born in Andong, South Korea, and now lives in Seoul. In 1996 she received the Sangsang Literary Award for her debut novel, *Niche of Green*. Her subsequent novels and short stories have received numerous literary awards, including the Hankook Ilbo Literary Award, Yi Sang Literary Prize, and the Oh Yeong-su Literature Award, among others. *Lemon* is her first novel to be published in English.

JANET HONG is a writer and translator based in Vancouver, Canada. She received the 2018 TA First Translation Prize and the 16th LTI Korea Translation Award for her translation of Han Yujoo's *The Impossible Fairy Tale*, which was also a finalist for both the 2018 PEN Translation Prize and the 2018 National Translation Award. Her recent translations include Ha Seong-nan's *Bluebeard's First Wife*, Ancco's *Nineteen*, and Keum Suk Gendry-Kim's *Grass*.

1/3   10 - 3
        Highlands - Women's Only

1/4   10-3
        Snowmass Bumps & Steeps
1/6   10-3
        Highlands - Women's Only

1/7   10 of 3
        Highlands Women's Only

1/8   10-3
        Snowmass Bumps & Steeps

1/9   10-3
        Highlands Bowl

Women's Edge
    2/6 $839
    2/13   4 days 10-3
    2/20
    3/4